**Novelization by Megan Stine
based on the screenplay by
Bill Kelly and Hugh Wilson
story by Bill Kelly**

A PARACHUTE BOOK
Parachute Publishing, L.L.C.
156 Fifth Avenue
New York, NY 10010

Printed in the U.S.A.
March 1999
ISBN: 1-57351-000-9
10 9 8 7 6 5 4 3 2 1

chapter one

Adam Webber stared at the long tunnel of the escape hatch.

"Do you think it's safe there?" he asked his mother.

"I don't know, dear," Helen Webber replied, biting her lip.

Adam's father had just ridden the elevator up the tunnel. Up to a place Adam had only heard about in stories. A place he'd only dreamed of—

The surface. The surface of Earth.

Adam's heart raced. This was amazing! He had spent his entire life underground. But if his father's mission was successful—if he found out that the surface of the Earth was safe again—

Adam might actually get to see what was up there!

Adam's parents had told him many times the story of why they lived underground. By now, Adam knew the story so well he could recite it by heart.

Before he was born, way back in 1962, his parents locked themselves in an underground bomb shelter—one his father had built in their backyard. They went underground because the Russians dropped a nuclear missile on California.

Calvin Webber calculated that it would take thirty-five years for the radiation from the bomb to reach safe levels on the planet. Before that time, there would be nothing but hideous mutants walking around on the surface. So he made sure he had thirty-five years' worth of food and water for himself, his wife, and little Adam—once he came along.

Life was good underground, Adam knew. It was safe. Secure. But something deep inside him wanted more. Something he was sure he could find on the surface. He longed to see the sun, the sky, mountains, oceans...all the things his mother had told him about since he was a tiny child. All the things he'd seen only in old photographs from the time before his parents went underground.

And now the day was finally here! He would finally get to see everything!

The sky. It must be amazing!

And fresh air. He'd never breathed it into his

lungs before. Or felt the sun on his bare skin. Or a breeze on his face.

Most of all, he'd never seen a girl. Well, other than his mother. In fact, he'd never seen any other *human beings* except his parents.

I hope they're not all mutants up there, Adam worried silently.

But he didn't know he had nothing to worry about at all. Russia never dropped a bomb on California. What Calvin Webber thought was a nuclear missile was really an experimental aircraft crashing in the Webbers' backyard.

There was no radiation. No fallout. No reason to stay underground.

Of course, just because life went on after 1962 didn't mean it went on without changes. In the years since then, *everything* had changed. Music. Clothes. Cars. The way people wore their hair. The way they talked to one another.

It was all totally different from the way Adam had been taught the world was.

Adam's world was filled with the music and clothes and rules that his parents had brought with them into the bomb shelter—from 1962. Things like Perry Como records. And bright green plaid shirts with brown pants. Roller *skates*—the kind that came with keys. Good table manners.

All the stuff that was popular in 1962.

As a kid, Adam's father taught him history,

French, German, geography, English, math, and science. What else was there to do hundreds of feet below the surface?

Adam loved every subject. But Calvin hadn't been able to teach him a thing about what it was like to be with a girl.

That's what Adam wanted to know. He'd been thinking about girls—dreaming about them—for a very long time now. Almost as long as he'd been wanting to see the sky.

And now that he was on the verge of actually meeting a girl, he had no idea how to handle it.

"Do you think it's safe?" he asked his mother again. She stood beside him at the rear hatchway, waiting for Calvin to return.

Helen shrugged. "Your father will be able to tell us soon."

Adam glanced at her, noticing how distracted she seemed. She's as eager to get to the surface as I am, he realized.

"Here he comes!" Helen declared, her voice cracking.

The elevator moved slowly down the long shaft. It bumped to a stop in front of Adam and Helen.

Adam held his breath, straining for the first glimpse of his father's face. What had he seen up there?

The door swung open, revealing a tall figure in a yellow rubber antiradiation suit. It looked sort of like a deep-sea diver's suit, with heavy boots and a bulky helmet.

Through the helmet's faceplate, Adam saw that his father's face was pale. Calvin stepped shakily off the elevator platform.

"Dad?" Adam asked anxiously. "Are you okay?"

Calvin pulled off the helmet without answering. His hair was soaked with sweat. He staggered to the kitchen table, breathing hard.

Adam gnawed his lower lip, worried. This looked bad.

"What happened?" Helen asked, taking a seat across from Calvin. Adam pulled out his own chair as quietly as he could.

"I'm going to give it to you straight," Calvin answered. "There's no point in beating around the bush."

He drew a deep, gasping breath. "The radiation levels are fine. And there were survivors after the blast," he announced. "But apparently we haven't locked ourselves in long enough. The fallout must have created a...a subspecies."

Adam stifled a gasp.

Calvin turned his somber gaze from Helen to Adam. "A subspecies...of mutants."

"Mutants?" Helen gulped.

Adam felt a chill. Mutants—just what he had been afraid of.

"It's not a pretty sight up there," Calvin went

on. "Society as we knew it has utterly collapsed. Some people eat out of garbage cans. Others throw up in the streets. Others wave guns around, and, Helen—there's something *terribly* wrong with the automobiles. And..." Calvin shook his head. "I can't tell you the rest," he finished in a low voice. "I just can't. Maybe some day."

Adam glanced at his mother, whose eyes were wide in shock.

"What do we do now?" she asked.

"We stay down here," Calvin said.

Adam slumped in his chair. No!

"For how long?" Helen demanded. "We've just about run out of all our supplies!"

"We'll make do," Calvin replied. "We've got the garden we've maintained down here—and the fish farm. I'm of the opinion that these mutants will eventually kill each other off. And then..."

Adam swallowed hard. Then he noticed his father's face. It was turning even paler. As if all the blood were draining out of it.

Calvin stood up and clutched his chest.

"Dad!" Adam cried.

"Oh, no!" Helen shouted. "Get him into the bedroom!"

Adam leaped up and raced around the table. He caught Calvin as he started to fall. Gently, carefully, Adam lifted his father and carried him to his bed.

Calvin lay still. His breath rasped in his throat. His face was gray. As Helen bustled around, Adam backed out of the room, shivering slightly.

His father had gone up to the surface, and now he was really sick. Things must be bad up there, Adam thought. Terribly bad.

chapter two

A few hours later, Adam and his mother huddled together in the space outside the bedroom.

"Is Dad going to be okay?" Adam asked. His face felt tight with worry.

"He seems to be doing all right," Helen whispered. "I don't know if he's had a heart attack or just a horrifying experience. But we need supplies—and I've got to stay here with him."

Adam knew what had to be done. He squared his shoulders.

"I'll go up," he volunteered. He gave his mother a look that said: Don't worry. I know it's dangerous up there, but I can handle it.

Inside, though, Adam wasn't so sure. What kind

of horrible creatures might be waiting for him?

He shook his head. It didn't matter, he decided. He needed to do this—for his parents.

Helen's eyes crinkled with worry, but she nodded at her son. "Yes, I'm afraid you'll have to go," she agreed. "We can't go on without the supplies."

"I'll be all right, Mom," Adam reassured her.

"Remember—just act normal," Helen said. "If anybody asks anything about you, simply say you're from out of town. And that you're in Los Angeles on business. All right?"

Adam nodded.

"I'm going to give you a shopping list, and some money," she continued. "We need just enough yacht batteries and diesel oil for fuel, and enough food to get us through the next year or two. You'll find most of these items at a *grocery* store or a *hardware* store. Got that?"

"Yes, ma'am." He mouthed the unfamiliar words. *Grocery. Hardware.*

"Let's get you packed, then," Helen said, heading toward Adam's room.

"Mom?" Adam asked as he followed her.

"Yes?"

"I was thinking that, uh...you know, while I was up there and all..." He stammered, trying to find a way to say what had been on his mind for so long.

Helen gazed at him quizically. "Go on, dear."

"Well, I thought maybe I could, you know...try

to meet a girl. I've, um, been thinking about that a little. Just these last...few years."

"Oh, Adam," Helen said, beaming. "It would be wonderful if you could find a girl. One who's not a mutant. And hopefully," she added, "someone who comes from Pasadena. Nothing against Valley girls, mind you, but in my day, the girls from Pasadena—I don't know—always just seemed a little...nicer. And I would think that most young ladies up there would be very anxious to meet a nice young man who lives in a safe fallout shelter."

Adam's heart leaped. Boy, I hope so, he thought. Because all I know about girls is what Mom taught me—to be polite and use good manners at all times.

"You think?" he asked.

"Oh, I should say so," Helen answered. "But you'd better keep that part—about the bomb shelter—a secret. At least until you know you can really trust the girl."

"Yes, ma'am," Adam replied. That made sense.

He hurried to his room and packed his clothes in a suitcase. Then he grabbed his most treasured possession—a cigar box his father had given him. Inside was a complete set of 1955 series baseball cards—in perfect condition. His father had collected them years before Adam was born.

There were also some old stock certificates his

father had given him to play with when he was a kid, a handmade sling-shot, and an old photograph of his parents in their backyard.

He tucked the box into his suitcase carefully, then closed the lid.

He glanced up when he heard his mother coming into his room. She carried a piece of paper and some cash in her hands.

"Here's the shopping list and three thousand dollars, which should take care of everything," she said solemnly. Adam saw that her forehead was still knit with worry.

His mother walked silently with him to the elevator. Adam hugged her.

Then he stepped into the elevator.

Well, here goes...*everything*, he thought.

And he punched the UP button.

chapter three

Adam gripped his suitcase tightly as he rode up to the surface. A red light in the exit hatchway glowed up through the cracks in the elevator shaft. It cast an eerie light on the dark space above.

Adam gazed up through the cracks and saw broken pieces of cement.

Weird, he thought. For a minute, he couldn't figure out what he was looking at. But then it became clear. Someone had built an entire building on top of his family's exit hatch. When his father went up to the surface earlier that day, the elevator had broken through the cement floor.

Of course. It made sense. After all, Adam's family had been underground for so long.

Things had to change.

The doors opened. Adam found himself standing inside a small, dingy building of some sort.

Was it a...restaurant?

He had seen pictures of restaurants in magazines. And old TV programs that his father had on film. So he had *some* idea how they should look.

But this was so different.

He gazed around, trying to make out what the place was supposed to be.

An old malt shop, he decided. Yes. That was it. There were old chrome stools, and a long counter that looked like a soda fountain. Maybe this was one of those fun hangouts for teenagers that he had seen in the films.

But now it was empty and dark. The windows were painted black. The furnishings were mostly gone.

There was a small grouping of flowers and candles, along with some costume jewelry, on the floor near the elevator shaft. It looked like some sort of shrine.

And then he saw the man.

His first human being—besides his family.

The man wore grubby clothes and had strange blue markings on his forehead. His hair was long and greasy, streaked with gray. He stood rocking back and forth, praying.

A mutant, Adam thought nervously. He has to

be, with those blue markings.

Then the man glanced up—and caught sight of Adam. His eyes opened wide.

Adam tensed. But instead of attacking him, the man fell to his knees and started crying.

Adam stared. He isn't quite as scary as I expected, he thought.

He put down his suitcase and cautiously approached the man.

"Are you all right?" he asked.

"Yes! Yes! Oh, yes, oh, yes!" the man moaned. "But where is the one who came last night—all in yellow?"

"All in yellow?" Adam repeated. Oh. His father's antiradiation suit. "That was my father."

"Oooohhhh! Of course! The father!" the man exclaimed. He bowed even lower, as if he were praying to Adam. He seemed to be trying to make himself as small and as humble as possible.

"Forgive me!" the man wailed. "Can you forgive me for my wasted life? Everything has been so awful!"

Awful? Adam thought. Yes. After the bomb, with all the radiation, life must have been horrible on the surface.

He bent down and put a hand on the man's shoulder.

"I *know* it's been terrible up here," Adam said in a comforting voice. "But it wasn't your fault. And now all the decay is over with and things are going to get better. You understand?"

"Yes." The man sniffled.

Adam glanced toward the door. He was impatient to get on his way. "I've got to go now," he announced.

"Of course you do. I'll stay here and pray," the man answered.

"Uh—right. That's always a good idea!" Adam said.

"Will you be back?" the man asked.

"Yes. I promise," Adam answered. He headed for the door.

This is it! he told himself. I am going outside!

Adam swung open the door. He stepped out into the street.

Yeow! He felt as if he'd been hit by lightning. The sensation of being outdoors was...shocking.

There was so much noise. Cars whizzing by at incredible speeds. Horns honking. Clattering truck wheels. Voices shouting.

And so much motion. The cars. People hurrying by—on foot, on bicycles. So many people!

But most of all, there was so much *light*.

Sunlight! It's so bright—so warm! he thought.

He stared at a patch of it on the arm of his coat. Then, slowly, he lifted his head and let his gaze move up to the sky.

"Ahhhhh!" Adam gasped.

It was bigger, more beautiful, more glorious than he had ever imagined.

Adam's throat tightened. His breaths came fast, but shallow. His knees felt weak.

It was just amazing!

"What?" a woman passing by asked. "What is it?"

"The sky!" Adam cried in total awe.

He pointed up at the clouds. At the blueness. At the amazing hugeness of it all.

How could it be so big? he wondered. So clear?

"The sky?" the woman repeated. She stared up.

"Up there!" Adam replied, pointing. Didn't she see it? Even *he* knew that the sky was directly overhead.

"I don't see anything!" the woman snapped.

Was she blind? Adam lowered his gaze to stare at her.

That's when he noticed the crowd gathering around him. Gazing up at the sky. Trying to figure out what all the fuss was about.

"What is it?" someone asked.

"He sees something up there," the woman replied.

"I have *never in my life* seen anything like this!" Adam cried out. "*Nothing even comes close!*"

"*I* see it, Mommy!" a child called proudly.

"Where? Where is it?" a man in the crowd asked.

Adam gazed around at the crowd. What strange people! They couldn't see the sky! Maybe they all see it so often, they don't even notice it anymore, he thought.

Oh, well. It didn't matter. Adam had to move on, anyway. He had things to do. And he wanted to see more of the world!

But first, he stared at the malt shop, so he'd remember where he was and how to get home. He made a mental note of the exterior. A chrome front, with an old broken neon sign over the entrance that read: MOM'S MALT SHOP.

Adam planted the picture firmly in his mind, then hurried down the street. As he neared the corner, he spotted a long vehicle filled with rows of seats. It was speeding toward the intersection.

A bus! Adam thought. His parents had told him about them, but he'd never been on one before. He just *had* to try it.

Adam stepped off the curb and walked to the middle of the wide street. He put up his hand. It seemed like the best way to signal the bus driver to stop.

SCREEEEECH!

The brakes squealed as the bus slammed to a stop just inches from Adam.

As he climbed the bus steps, he heard the driver cursing. "That was a dumb stunt, buddy!" the driver yelled at Adam.

What's wrong with him? Adam wondered. It was so strange to hear someone yelling. And sounding so angry. His parents *never* did that.

Adam pulled one of his hundred-dollar bills out of his pocket and handed it to the driver.

"I'm sorry, but I don't have any change," he said. "Can you...?"

"Just sit down!" the driver shouted, not even looking at Adam. "Sit and get out of my face!"

No wonder Dad was so shaken up when he came to the surface, Adam thought. If everyone up here yells like that, it's definitely a scary place.

Adam plopped down in a seat. He smiled at the person next to him. The young man was dressed in raggedy clothes. His hair was wild and greasy and his eyes were sort of...well, *weird*. Glazed over.

The bus lurched away from the curb. "Whoa!" Adam cried. He grabbed on to the pole in front of him to keep himself from sliding off the seat.

"Hey! We're moving!" he shouted joyfully. Being on a bus was wild! So fast!

"Yikes! Hold on, everybody! Wow!" Adam cried.

The young guy next to Adam rolled his eyes.

But Adam didn't care. All he knew was that this was amazing. Life. Up top. On the surface. Amazing—even if it was a little scary.

"So this is public transportation, eh?" he said to everyone on the bus. "My dad and I studied it.

Would you happen to know where a grocery store is? Guess not. Well, I don't see anyone throwing up or waving a gun around." Adam turned to the guy next to him. "Do you have a gun?"

The guy gave him a startled glance, then nodded.

Wow, Adam thought. Dad was right about how society had changed after the bomb. Maybe *everyone* had a gun!

"Well, thanks for not waving it. And for not vomiting, for that matter!" Adam said politely.

He glanced out the window. They were passing a building with a big red-and-white sign that said: SUPERFOOD.

"Isn't that a grocery store over there?" Adam asked.

The guy next to him didn't answer.

"Driver!" Adam stood up. "Please stop this bus! I would like to get off!"

The bus driver didn't turn his head. The bus speeded up slightly.

"Driver!" Adam called again. "I'd like to get off here!"

"Let him off!" an elderly woman near the front yelled. "Can't you see he's loony?"

"Yeah," another man called. "Get him out of here!"

Grumbling, the driver stepped on the brake. The bus came to a halt and Adam swung down the steps. A smile spread across his face as he marched up to the supermarket.

What an adventure!

He gasped as he approached the glass doors. They opened *automatically*!

Adam stepped back and forth for a few moments, opening them them just by passing the electronic sensor.

After a while he got tired of that and decided to walk *inside* the store.

Wow! Adam's mouth fell open. The checkout lanes! The price scanners, the conveyor belts—his father never told him about any of that stuff!

But he couldn't stand there all day. He had work to do.

He glanced around and noticed people taking carts and wheeling them down the aisles. Adam did the same. He put his suitcase in his cart, then headed down an aisle, trying to absorb it all.

But there were so many choices. Almost too many! He didn't know where to look first.

Finally he found his way toward the meat counter and pressed the buzzer for service.

A fat man in a stained white butcher's coat appeared at the window a few moments later. "Help you?" he asked.

"Good afternoon." Be polite and friendly! Adam thought. He offered his hand to shake. "I'm Adam Webber."

For some reason, the butcher looked surprised. He took Adam's hand reluctantly.

"Uh, hi," he said.

"How much are beef patties?" Adam asked, naming the first item on his shopping list.

"Fresh or frozen?" the butcher replied.

"Frozen. We only eat fresh *fish*. We never have fresh meat," Adam explained.

"Never?" The butcher squinted at Adam.

"No, never."

"Well, the three pound box of twelve frozen all-beef patties is six-thirty," the butcher said.

Adam's eyes grew wide. "You mean six *dollars* and thirty cents?" Was that a joke? He couldn't believe the price. It was so much higher than his mother had told him to expect.

"Does that seem high?" the butcher asked.

"High?" Adam sputtered. "Well, um—yes. I mean, if I needed four hundred patties...that would be, uh...two hundred and seven dollars or thereabouts. Just for the beef! However, my mother only gave me three thousand dollars for *everything*! Yacht batteries, pipe tobacco, diesel oil, toilet paper—the works!"

The butcher took a small step backward. He looked as if he would rather be somewhere else. Maybe he's got a lot of work to do, Adam thought. I'd better not keep him.

"Sir, could you tell me what aisle contains the

diesel oil?" Adam asked.

"Diesel oil? In a grocery store? What are you, some kind of a nut?" the butcher demanded.

Adam frowned. "Excuse me?"

The butcher shrugged. "Look, maybe you could call a meat wholesaler and ask him to deliver the patties."

"Why, yes! That's a very good idea!" Adam said.

He started to smile and thank the man for the suggestion. Yes. He'd have them delivered home!

But—wait a minute, Adam thought.

His heart started to pound. Sweat broke out across his forehead.

It was a good plan—except for one thing.

He didn't have a clue which direction home was.

Oh, no, Adam thought. *I'm lost!*

chapter four

In a panic, Adam hurried out of the supermarket—into the twilight.

No! How could the sun be setting so fast?

Adam approached the curb. Horns honked at him. He covered his ears. Blazing headlights hit him in the face. He covered his eyes. All around him, people were rushing everywhere. Brushing roughly past him.

Out of the corner of his eye, Adam caught sight of a strange structure with a roof but no walls. BUS STOP, a sign beside it said.

Yes! He felt a surge of relief. The bus! He had to get back on the bus.

But which one had he taken before?

He wasn't sure.

All he knew was that he had to get back to where he came from—back to Mom's Malt Shop. The place they'd built on top of his family's bomb shelter.

Finally, he stepped up to the bus stop and picked one. Any one. Anywhere had to be better than this crowded corner.

He stepped on the bus and reached into his pocket. Oh, no. He still had only the roll of hundred-dollar bills his mother gave him.

He peeled off a hundred-dollar bill from his wad and handed it to the driver.

"Would you please take this?" he begged. "I know it's too much, but it's all I have."

The driver looked Adam up and down.

"Are you kidding me?" he asked.

"No, sir," Adam replied. "Please. I need to get on this bus."

The driver grabbed the bill and quickly slipped it into his pocket. Adam noticed a funny smile spread across his face.

"Thank you, sir," Adam said. "*You* are a good person."

"Yeah, *right*," the bus driver mumbled.

Adam staggered down the aisle of the lurching bus, gripping the overhead handrail with all his might.

He couldn't believe how jerky the bus felt. He

lunged into the only remaining free seat, by the back door.

Please let this bus take me back to the malt shop, Adam thought. He watched out the window for some familiar sight.

But by then the sun had totally set. And everything looked so different in the dark.

Adam couldn't recognize anything!

He felt his throat beginning to close. As if he might cry.

He swallowed hard, and told himself to toughen up. Men don't cry, he reminded himself. That's what Dad always says.

The bus slowed, then stopped. A young woman got on and staggered down the crowded aisle.

Adam stood up immediately to offer her his seat, as his father had taught him.

"Miss?" he said, gesturing toward the empty space.

She smiled and sat down gratefully. Adam smiled back. He began to feel a little better.

He gazed out the window into the darkness, trying to spot the one landmark in the whole world that was familiar to him. Mom's Malt Shop.

Apartment buildings, clothing boutiques, and restaurants flew by.

But none of them looked right!

I'm never going to find it, he thought.

And then, there it was!

The stainless steel front and everything!

Adam didn't want to be rude—but he was in a hurry. He pushed his way to the front of the bus as politely as he could.

"I've got to get off the bus!" he cried. "I've got to get off now!"

"Sure, buddy," the driver said, giving Adam that same weird smile. "Whatever you want." He stepped on the brake.

When the bus stopped, Adam climbed off and began trying to cross the busy street. The only problem was, there didn't seem to be a traffic light. Or a crosswalk.

Oh, Adam thought. Maybe this is a highway. Mom and Dad told me about those. How do people get across them?

Adam darted in and out among the speeding cars. Drivers slammed on their brakes and honked angrily. But he didn't care. He had one thought: Get home!

Finally he reached the far side of the street and hurried toward the malt shop.

I made it! he thought. I'm not lost anymore.

But as he approached the building, his throat began to tighten up again.

Wait a minute. This place looked too...clean. Too new. Neon signs blinked in the malt shop's windows.

DINER, Adam read. TWENTY-FOUR HOURS.

The lump in his throat grew.

This wasn't right.

I *am* lost, Adam realized, feeling the panic build up again.

"I'm not going to cry," he mumbled to himself, trying to stay calm despite his fear. "Don't cry. That's the first thing. Just walk along...until you think of something."

Walking seemed to help. At least for a moment. He kept his feet moving, and pretty soon he began to notice things that caught his attention.

A mannequin in a store window, wearing a tiny bikini. A billboard, with an advertisement for underwear.

And...

"Oh, wow, a *dog*!" Adam exclaimed. He rushed up to a woman who was walking her medium-sized scruffy brown dog.

It wasn't a special dog, Adam realized. Not a pure breed or anything. Just an old mutt on a leash. But it was his first real, live dog. He could barely contain his excitement.

Adam stooped down to get on the dog's level. It was so amazing to stare into a face covered with...fur!

"Can I touch him?" Adam asked eagerly.

"Sure," the woman answered, smiling.

Adam knelt on the sidewalk with a feeling of sheer joy. It was the first animal he'd ever petted in his life. Other than the fish his father raised in the shelter.

"I like his face," Adam said. He smiled at the dog. Somehow, he felt much happier than he had a moment earlier.

At last, Adam stood and thanked the woman. Then he gazed around to see where he was. The shop window right in front of him displayed a sign that said: COMIC BOOKS AND BASEBALL CARDS— BOUGHT, SOLD, & TRADED.

Hmmm, Adam thought. Baseball cards? I have some of those.

He thought for another second. Maybe this was a way to solve one of his problems, he decided. Specifically, the problem of not having any change smaller than a hundred-dollar bill.

He glanced at his suitcase. Inside was the cigar box with his entire baseball card collection. Adam decided to go in.

Behind the counter sat a guy about Adam's age. The guy barely glanced up from his magazine when Adam walked in.

Adam approached the counter. "Hello," he said.

"Hi," the guy answered, still reading.

Adam cleared his throat. "The name is Adam Webber and I see you buy baseball cards," he began. "And although the ones I have are a lot older than the ones in the window, I was hoping you still might be interested."

"Older?" The guy glanced up sharply at Adam. Then he lowered his gaze to the cigar box Adam had placed on the counter. His eyes narrowed.

"Uh, hi," he said. "I'm Jerry."

"Pleased to meet you, Jerry," Adam said, offering his hand to shake.

Jerry didn't take Adam's hand. His eyes remained focused on the box. Adam put his hand down and flipped open the lid to show Jerry his complete set of 1955 series baseball cards.

Jerry's mouth opened. He sort of moaned.

Adam glanced at him curiously. "Does that mean you like the cards?" he asked.

Jerry instantly covered his mouth and coughed.

"Uh, they're n-n-nice," he stammered. "How...how much do you want for the Willie Mays, rookie season?"

"I was thinking of selling them all," Adam announced.

"Really? No kidding?" Jerry's face went through a series of expressions that confused Adam.

Maybe he doesn't think much of my cards, Adam guessed. But he doesn't want to hurt my feelings.

Jerry started to flip through the cards.

"See, my problem is, all I have are hundred-dollar bills, and I need something smaller," Adam explained. "Ones, fives, tens. Like that."

Jerry narrowed his eyes. "That's a joke, right?" he said.

"No," Adam replied. "I'm serious. I'm sorry, have I done something wrong?"

"No. No!" Jerry said. A strange smile spread across his lips. A lot like that bus driver's smile, Adam thought.

Jerry cleared his throat. "You've, uh, you've come to the right place. Tell you what. I'll give you five hundred dollars in small bills for the whole box."

"Oh, that would be wonderful!" Adam exclaimed gratefully.

"Well, we're here to help!" Jerry replied.

Suddenly, from the back of the small store, Adam heard a woman's voice. He didn't catch what she said. It was a loud exclamation of some sort.

Jerry's head snapped up, and he shot an angry glance in the woman's direction.

Adam turned too.

And found himself gazing at the most beautiful girl he had ever seen.

She was blond, with big blue eyes and rosy cheeks. And the most amazing little chin. And a kind of intoxicating tilt to her head.

The moment Adam saw her, he knew he wanted to know her better. Stand beside her. Listen to every word she said.

He felt dizzy and excited and—totally in *love*.

This is it, Adam thought. This is the girl I've come to the surface to find. This is my future wife!

I wonder if she's from Pasadena?

Who *is* this nerd? Eve Cosovak wondered. She headed toward the front counter of the baseball card store where she worked.

She stared hard at him, checking out his lemon-yellow plaid shirt, his brush-cut hair, his worn, out-of-date shoes. The whole package was unbelievable.

This guy looked like something out of the fifties! The lamest part of the fifties. Definitely not the Elvis part.

He was obviously a hick, Eve decided. A guy from so far out in the sticks that he had no idea what was happening.

And he *certainly* had no idea what his baseball cards were worth. He was about to practically give them away.

Eve stepped up to the front counter with her hands on her hips. She shot her boss, Jerry, a glare that said: Don't even try it. Don't try to rip this guy off for all he's worth, or I'll make your life totally miserable. Understand?

"I'm workin' here, Evie-poo," Jerry said in a fake, syrupy voice. "Don't mess me up, babe."

Eve ignored Jerry and greeted the dweeby guy instead.

"How are you?" she asked. She kept her voice even, no-nonsense, and full of attitude. Around here you had to keep your guard up and make sure people understood that no one was going to put anything over on you.

"*Bonjour, mademoiselle!*" the guy replied, sounding like something out of an old movie. He gave a little bow.

Eve tried not to laugh. She picked up the Willie Mays baseball card lying on top of the box. She stuck it in his face.

"You have any idea what this one card alone is worth?" she asked him.

"No, ma'am."

Ma'am? Oh, wow. He was an even bigger hick than she thought. Someone had to save him from himself!

"It's worth six thousand dollars," she said, tossing it back into the cigar box.

"Six thousand dollars!" The hick's eyes grew huge.

"Yep." Eve folded her arms.

Out of the corner of her eye, she saw Jerry fuming.

"Terrific," he said, spitting the word at Eve angrily. She knew what he really meant: Thanks for totally ruining my golden deal.

Ignoring Jerry, Eve picked up the cigar box. She practically shoved it at the hick.

"Now, I want you to climb back on that turnip truck you came into town on, and get out of here," she ordered him.

"I came on a bus," the guy corrected her.

Jerry rolled his eyes and slapped the counter. "You're fired, Eve!" he snapped. "You know that?"

"No, Jerry," Eve snapped back. "I quit!"

She spun around and headed toward the back of the store to get her bag.

"Oh, no!" Jerry called after her. "I fired you! Just like the hair salon guy and the Chevy dealer! You know why you can't keep a single job, Eve? Because you can't keep your mouth shut! That's why!"

Yeah, whatever, Eve thought. Bug off.

She marched toward the front of the store again, ready to storm out.

As she neared the counter, she noticed the hick guy leaning over it. He put his hand firmly on Jerry's arm and scowled into Jerry's face.

"Sir?" the hick said. "I would *really* appreciate it if you wouldn't use that tone of voice with a lady."

Eve stared at him, speechless. Was this guy for real? He seemed too old-fashioned to be true.

He really needed help. In fact, this guy needed some kind of keeper.

Eve took the guy by the arm and led him away from the counter. "Come on," she told him. "I'll walk you to the corner."

"Yes, ma'am. By the way, my name is Adam," the hick said.

"Hah!" Jerry shrieked. "Adam and Eve! The perfect match! I hope you two will be very happy together!"

Rolling her eyes, Eve led Adam to the street. Outside, the traffic on the boulevard was buzzing. She walked briskly, leading Adam toward the corner bus stop, where she figured she could dump him safely.

"You be careful with those baseball cards. You hear me?" she said to Adam.

"Yes, ma'am," he said obediently. Eve wished he would stop staring at her. He looked like some kind of eager puppy.

"And stop with the *ma'am* stuff," she snapped. "Do I look like a ma'am to you?"

"Um..."

Eve tried not to laugh. The confused expression on his face was pathetic.

"Did you just lose your job because of me?" Adam asked, sounding guilty and grateful all at once.

"Forget it," Eve said quickly. "I was sick of working for that jerk anyway." She pointed toward the corner. "You can catch the bus there. You should be back in Mayberry by morning."

"Mayberry?" Adam looked puzzled.

"Yeah, Mayberry," Eve repeated impatiently.

"You know, from the TV show? Big hit in the sixties? Reruns all the time on *Nick at Nite*?"

Eve waited for Adam to nod, but saw only a blank look on his face.

Wow! What planet is this guy *from*, anyway? she wondered.

She stared at his clothes.

Then again, maybe he's an alien, she reasoned.

Either way, she'd done her good deed for the day. Enough was enough.

Without another word, she turned and walked off in the opposite direction as fast as she could.

"Wait!" Adam called.

Eve stopped. What *now*?

She turned around and waited.

"I'm lost," Adam admitted sheepishly. "I don't know where I am and I'm getting pretty scared—because I don't know where to go or what to do!"

"You're *lost*?" Eve rolled her eyes. This was becoming more unbelievable every second.

"Let me guess," she said, not even trying to hide the fact that she was making fun of him. "This is your first visit to L.A. You're staying somewhere over in Hollywood because, like an idiot, you thought that would be an exciting place to stay. Right so far?"

Adam hesitated.

"And don't lie to me!" Eve added. "I can *always* tell when someone is lying! I have this thing."

"Uh, okay," Adam said. "You—you're right."

All right! Eve thought. Can I figure people out, or what?

"So you got on a bus, and before you knew it, you were out here in the San Fernando Valley without a clue," she went on. "Correct again?"

"Again," Adam agreed, nodding hard.

"And while I'm on this psychic roll," Eve went on, "I predict that you are staying at the Hollywood Holiday Inn. Naturally. Just nod if I've hit it squarely on the button."

Adam nodded again, grinning.

Eve's eyes popped open wide. "You're kidding! Wow! I *am* pretty good!" she exclaimed.

"You're *great*," Adam said dreamily. "You're absolutely wonderful."

Eve took one look at the goofy expression on his face and knew it was time to go. The *last* thing she needed just then was to get stuck with a hick weirdo who had a crush on her!

"Well, thank you," she said. She clapped her hands together briskly. "Okay, now I know which buses you need to take. First you—"

"Do you own a car?" Adam interrupted her.

She shook her head fast. "I'm not taking you there, sweetie," she said. "Rule number one: No strangers in the car."

"I don't have a gun," Adam offered innocently.

Eve eyed him suspiciously. What kind of crazy-person announcement was *that*? A gun? Who even *thought* that he might have a gun?

This guy is too weird, Eve decided. I am out of here.

"Get away from me!" she shouted. "I mean it!"

She turned and hurried around the corner toward the parking lot where her car was parked.

She didn't even stop when she heard him calling after her.

"Wait! Please, wait!" Adam called.

No way, Eve thought. Consider me out of your life—for good!

chapter five

No! Adam thought. The most beautiful girl I've ever seen is disappearing around the corner.

He couldn't let her get away!

Besides—he was still lost. Totally lost. How was he going to find his way home without her help?

He turned and ran after her.

"Wait! Please wait! I'll make a deal with you!" he called to Eve. "I'll give you a Willie Mays card if you'll take me to the hotel! He's yours—free!"

For an instant, Eve looked as if she wasn't going to stop. Then she turned around and threw up her hands.

"I told you already!" she snapped. "He's worth

six thousand dollars!"

"So what?" Adam shot back. "I've got six of him!"

Eve's jaw dropped.

"You've got *six* Willie Mays, rookie season?" she asked.

Adam nodded and pulled more baseball cards out of his pockets. "And this many DiMaggios and Robinsons." He paused, smiling. "I was holding these out."

Pretty smart, huh? he wanted to add. But he decided that would be too conceited.

Eve cocked her head to one side. "For six thousand dollars, all I have to do is drive you to your hotel?"

"Yes,"

"And that's it?"

"Yes," he repeated.

"And I don't have to take a physical in your spacecraft or anything?" she snapped.

My spacecraft? Wow, Adam thought. Things really *have* changed since 1962!

"No, ma'am!" Adam said quickly. "I mean, no!"

"Okay. You got a deal. Get in." Eve unlocked her car.

Great, Adam thought. His spirits immediately lifted. At least for the next fifteen or twenty minutes, he would still be with Eve. Sitting right next to her. In her car!

And she was taking him to a hotel. A place he could sleep for the night. He felt a little safer, knowing that he wouldn't have to wander around on the streets by himself. Maybe he'd still be lost, but he'd be lost in a hotel room. He wouldn't be out in the cold.

Adam's heart started pumping with excitement as he walked around and opened the passenger door.

My first car ride, he thought. I wonder if it will be more fun than the bus.

He read the name on Eve's car and frowned. It said Geo.

A Geo? What was that?

It was very small compared to the cars he'd seen in his father's magazines. And it was dirty. It looked as if it hadn't been washed in a long time.

Adam climbed in, first moving some crumpled papers, empty cups, and a hairbrush that were cluttering up the passenger seat.

"Buckle up," Eve ordered him as she fastened her own seat belt.

Adam watched what she did and copied it.

I wonder why we have to be strapped in? he thought. Does this thing really go *that* fast?

A moment later, Eve put the key in the ignition and floored the gas pedal. The car zipped into traffic with a jerk.

Whoa! Adam thought. He gripped the armrest

and the seat belt for dear life.

He glanced at the speedometer. Wow! They were flying! *Thirty* miles per hour! He couldn't believe it.

For the next few minutes, he didn't know where to look first. The dashboard was fascinating, with all the lights and dials. But the view out the window was pretty exciting too. Cars seemed to zoom past him at unbelievable speeds.

Was it really safe to be going so fast?

Oh, man, Adam thought. His heart pounded as he checked the speedometer again. Now they were going *fifty* miles an hour!

Eve flipped on the radio. Music blared out of it so loud it vibrated through Adam's whole body. Adam clamped his hands over his ears.

"Stop it!" Eve complained. "Everybody who rides with me does that."

Okay, Adam thought, wanting to be polite. He uncovered his ears. But he couldn't stop staring at the radio.

The sound was so harsh. What was it anyway? Not like any music *he'd* ever heard.

Eve glanced over. Adam saw her gaze land on his hand, which was gripping the seat belt. His knuckles were turning white.

"So...Mister Andretti," she said. "Your first time on the freeway?"

"It's Webber. Adam Webber," he corrected her.

"I *know* that," Eve said. "You introduced your-self in the card shop, for Pete's sake!"

"Then why did you call me Andretti?" Adam asked. He frowned, confused. "Mario Andretti?"

"Race car driver? Speed demon? Winner of the Indy 500 a zillion times in a row?"

Adam shrugged.

"You just don't look too comfortable in this car," she explained finally. "It was a *joke*. Forget it."

Oh, Adam thought. A joke. She was making fun of me. Swell.

Eve let out an exasperated sigh. Then she reached for the radio controls and started flipping around the dial. Suddenly, on one of the stations, familiar sounds came drifting out of the car speak-ers. Adam recognized them instantly.

Eve flipped past the station.

"Wait! Wait!" Adam blurted out.

Eve slammed on the brakes. "What is it?" she asked, alarmed.

"It's *Perry*!" Adam crooned.

"Perry?"

"Perry Como! You had him! Go back! Go back!" Adam pointed to the radio.

"Okay, okay!" Eve shot him a worried expres-sion. She punched up the station with the Perry Como song. "How's that?"

Adam's shoulders instantly relaxed. Finally.

Something he recognized. Even if it *was* only a song.

Eve jerked the wheel and cut in and out of two lanes. She squealed up the exit ramp and zoomed onto a side street.

Adam clung to his seat belt in sheer terror. "Gee-zooie! You'd better slow down!" he cried.

"I can't help it," Eve teased. "Perry Como does this to me. I just get *so* cranked!"

She's making fun of me again, Adam thought with a small cringe.

But so what? So what if she didn't like his music? It didn't matter.

She was still the most beautiful, wonderful girl in the world.

A few minutes later, the little car pulled up to the front of the Hollywood Holiday Inn. Eve skidded to a quick stop.

Whoa! Adam thought. He felt as if he'd just been on the ride of his life. The speed! The sights! He gazed at all the lights and people on Hollywood Boulevard.

He couldn't take it all in. He slumped back in his seat with a deep, satisfied sigh and a goofy grin on his face.

"Card, please," Eve demanded, holding out her hand. "End of service."

Adam happily pulled the Willie Mays baseball card out of his pocket and handed it to Eve.

"That was wonderful," he mumbled. "I've never felt anything like that in my life."

Of course there are a *whole lot* of things I've never heard, felt, seen, tasted, or done in my whole life, Adam thought. This was just one of them.

"Yeah. Same here," Eve cracked. Then she gestured toward the backseat. "Don't forget your suitcase."

"Right," Adam said.

He hopped out the car, suitcase in hand, and then leaned down into the window to say one more thing to Eve.

"You know..." he began.

She peeled away from the curb without listening to the rest of his sentence. Leaving him standing there. Alone.

With a sigh, he turned toward the hotel. Then he walked into the lobby and marched up to the registration desk.

"Good evening. I want to stay at this hotel," he announced to the desk clerk.

Good job, he congratulated himself. He'd handled that very well.

"Fill this out, please," the desk clerk replied, pushing a registration form in Adam's direction. "And I'll a need a card."

"A card?"

"Yes, sir."

Strange, Adam thought. I wonder how he knew I had baseball cards?

The hotel bellboy opened the door to Adam's deluxe room. Adam stared in amazement as he pointed out all the features inside.

There was a telephone with buttons on it. Wow! The phone in his parents' bomb shelter had a dial. And it didn't work anyway.

And the television—his father always projected film reels onto their nonworking TV screen. Adam had never seen *actual* TV before.

Then there was something the bellboy called a "remote." And a "room service menu." Adam had no idea what those were.

"Well, thank you very much," Adam said. "You've been very, very nice."

He held out his hand to shake.

The bellboy smiled. "Thank you," he said, grinning.

"No. Thank *you*," Adam insisted.

The bellboy glanced at his palm and frowned. For some reason he seemed disappointed.

That's strange, Adam thought. I *said* thank you. What more does he expect?

The bellboy scowled at Adam and headed toward the door.

"Well...good night," the bellboy called.

"Good night," Adam called back. "Sleep tight.

Don't let the bedbugs bite! That's what my mom always says..."

Mom.

As soon as he said the word, he felt himself begin to choke up. I wonder how she is, he thought. I wonder *where* she is.

Suddenly he realized how very far away from home he was. An enormous feeling of loneliness washed over him.

"...my mom, who I'm really beginning to miss," Adam told the bellboy, his voice cracking. "It's my first night away from home. My first night up on top."

"Up on top? You mean up here on the twelfth floor?" the bellboy wondered. He gave Adam a strange, questioning stare.

"Uh...yes," Adam said, quickly covering his mistake. Mom had told him not to reveal anything about the bomb shelter. Not to strangers. "Yes. Up here on the twelfth floor. Good night."

"Good night," the bellboy called.

When the bellboy was gone, Adam gazed around the room. It was all so...fascinating! Especially the television. It took a little while to figure out how it worked. But finally he hit a button on the thing the bellboy had called the "remote."

Bingo! The TV came on.

He sat down on the edge of the bed.

Color! Color TV! This was amazing!

How do they *do* that? Adam wondered.

Twelve hours later, long past when the sun came up the next morning, Adam was still sitting there watching television. He couldn't help it. It was unbelievably hypnotic.

The only thing that jolted him out of his TV trance was the ringing of the telephone beside his bed.

Adam stared at it. Lifted the receiver. And listened for a long time.

There was silence on the other end.

I wonder how this works? he thought.

Finally he spoke.

"Ummm...yes?"

"Hi," a voice on the other end said. "This is Eve, the woman from the baseball card store. Remember me?"

Remember her? Was she kidding? *Of course* he remembered her! He'd been thinking about her, off and on, all night.

There wasn't anyone on television who seemed as nice or as interesting or as beautiful as Eve.

"Yes! Hello!" Adam said eagerly.

Boy, oh, boy! he thought. Was he glad to hear from her! "Hot diggity dog! Thank you for calling me on the telephone!"

"Good grief." Eve sounded sort of put off. "I'm

calling from downstairs. In the lobby."

"You are?" He smiled broadly. This was great! "I'll be right down." He hung up the phone.

When he reached the lobby, Eve was standing near a bank of house phones. She wore a short black skirt that showed off most of her long, smooth, sun tanned legs.

Adam tried not to stare. It wouldn't be polite to stare at a woman's legs. At least he knew *that* much about living on the surface!

"I am so glad to see you!" he gushed. "I thought I'd never see you again!"

"Okay, down, boy," Eve said. "Look, here's the deal. I sold your Willie Mays this morning for five-seven—which is three short of what I said it was worth. But, hey..."

She stopped mid-sentence and stared at Adam's hand. He had clamped it over his mouth.

"Why are you doing that?" she asked.

"I haven't brushed yet," Adam admitted.

Eve rolled her eyes. "Oh, what a catastrophe! Okay. Anyhow, I don't feel right about this baseball card thing. So I'm just going to take a sales commission of one thousand dollars, which is *also* not fair—but too bad. And therefore the remainder is yours..."

She took a wad of money out of her bag and handed it to him.

"...some of which is in small bills because I

know how much trouble you have making change," she went on. "Anyhow, that's it. Take the money."

Adam felt too entranced by her presence to say anything. And besides, he didn't want to uncover his mouth. He silently took the money, staring at her clear blue eyes the whole time.

"And I'll see you around," Eve said, heading for the door.

"Wait, Eve, please!" he called, following her. "Wait!"

"Please don't follow me," she said, not breaking stride. "Just don't do it."

Don't follow her? Oh, no, Adam thought, slowing down.

For half a second, he was about to do what he was told. Just as he had always done at home. Besides, it wouldn't be polite to follow a lady if she didn't want your company, would it?

That's what his mother always told him.

But Mom wasn't here right now, was she?

No! He had to make his own decisions.

And he decided to take a chance.

Adam followed Eve boldly, keeping up with her, chasing her all the way out the door and down the street.

"I knew this would happen!" Eve complained. "You're like a stray dog!"

"Can't you please, please just talk to me for

one second?" Adam asked.

Eve made an exasperated clicking sound with her tongue. "Okay!"

They both stopped walking.

"I should have taken the money and run!" Eve muttered to herself. "That's what Troy told me to do! But do I listen? No!"

"Troy?" Adam asked. He felt a lump in his throat. "Is he your husband? Or...a...boyfriend?"

"No."

Adam tilted his head up to heaven and closed his eyes. "Thank-Q!" he said softly, imitating his father's favorite way of saying the phrase.

"Oh, *stop* that! You even talk like a nerd. Man!" Eve scolded. "Listen, I know you like me. I can tell. But you know what? A lot of guys like me. Well—not *me*, exactly. It's more like the legs or the body or the hair. Or some combination of the above."

Adam felt a mixture of tender emotions washing over him. Boy, was she interesting. She seemed so...so alive. So smart. So unafraid to say whatever she was thinking right then.

And she was right about so many things. She seemed to *know* everything!

But she was wrong about one thing. About the reason guys liked her. It wasn't the legs or the body or the hair—although they were great all right.

"I think it's the eyes," he said sweetly.

Eve just stared at him blankly. "The eyes. Okay. An eye man. Whatever. Anyhow, it *never* works out," Eve said. "Not that *you* even need to know that." She paused. "You look horrible, by the way," she said more kindly. "What have you been doing?"

"Watching television. In color!"

"Hey, no kidding! In color?" Her voice was mocking, but Adam couldn't entirely figure out why.

"Well, so long," she said, moving toward the parking garage.

Adam didn't follow her. He just stood his ground and called out, "*Why* does it never work out?"

"What?" she asked, turning.

"Why does it never work out? You and...guys?" he explained.

"Why? Who knows!" Eve sputtered.

Adam didn't budge. He just waited for a serious answer.

"Okay, if you promise to leave me alone, I'll tell you," she said.

"Okay," he agreed.

"It never works out because I'm into legs and bodies and hair *myself*. That's why. So I wind up with guys who are very good-looking but even more shallow than I am. Okay? Now, if you'll excuse me, I have to go find another low-paying, demeaning job."

She turned to leave again.

But Adam was having a flash of inspiration. An idea! And a pretty good one, too.

"Why not go to work for me?" he called out.

Eve stopped. But she didn't turn around.

"Doing what?" she asked scornfully.

"Selling my baseball cards," Adam explained. "And helping me buy enough food and supplies to fill several large trucks."

Eve turned her head. "Food and supplies? Who for?" she asked, frowning. "Like a charity thing?"

"Well..." Adam hated to lie. He had been brought up better than that. But he couldn't tell her the truth. Not about the fallout shelter. Not until he knew her well enough to trust her.

"Ummm..." he stalled.

"How long would you need me for?" Eve asked. She still sounded suspicious.

"Two weeks," Adam said.

"To help starving people?"

"No. It's for my mom and dad," he admitted honestly.

"Duh." Eve rolled her eyes. "Okay, you don't have to be a comedian. What's the pay?"

"What's fair?" Adam asked.

"I've got to make at least a thousand a week," she said.

Adam's face lit up. A thousand a week? He could afford that—now that he knew what the baseball cards were worth!

"It's a deal!" he exclaimed.

Eve's mouth fell open. "Really?" she gasped after a moment.

"Really!" Adam confirmed.

His heart skipped a beat when he thought about how much fun this was going to be. Spending all day, every day, with Eve. Shopping with Eve. Riding with Eve.

He could hardly wait to start!

chapter six

"Stay here while I change," Adam said. "I'll be right back." He hurried away.

Eve watched him walk back into the lobby of the Hollywood Holiday Inn. As soon as he was out of sight, she shook her head.

Did she just agree to work for this...this *nerd*? This helpless *creature*? This guy who looked like a cross between a farm boy and a character on *Saturday Night Live*?

"What am I doing?" she muttered as she waited for Adam to return.

"You're losing it, Eve," she told herself. "Losing your marbles. Big time."

When Adam hit the lobby ten minutes later,

every head in the place turned to stare at him.

Whoa! Eve thought, trying to comprehend what he was wearing. It was the ugliest combination of shirt and pants she had ever seen in her life.

This guy must be buying his clothes at a Goodwill Store—one that hadn't received any donations since the early sixties!

Adam was wearing a pair of brown polyester pants that were about four inches too short, and a pale blue and green plaid pullover shirt with a V-neck and wide, pointy collar.

Eve tried to remember if those clothes had *ever* been in style. Ever.

Nope, she decided. No way. They couldn't have been.

She shook her head and reminded herself that she was making a thousand bucks a week. For that kind of money, she could put up with a lot.

Even a fashion felony like this.

"Okay, cowboy, let's go," she said, leading Adam to her grungy little car.

The two of them hit the road, and Eve checked out Adam's shopping list.

Whoa! she thought.

"First item of business: We rent a U-Haul truck to cart the stuff around in," she told him. "Because this shopping list is gigantic. Really, really gigantic."

Once they had the truck, they drove it down to

the marina.

"Why would someone need *twenty* yacht batteries?" the manager at the marina asked Eve as his men loaded the batteries into the U-Haul truck.

Good question, Eve thought. Because supposedly they were getting all this stuff for starving people—right? And starving people didn't usually have yachts. Right? At least, not as far as she knew.

She stared at Adam, who stood a little ways away, thanking the men who were doing all the heavy lifting.

"I just work for the guy," she said finally with a shrug.

"Yeah, but who does *he* work for?" the marina manager asked.

Another good question, Eve thought. But she didn't know.

After that, the questions just kept piling up.

Like how come, at the discount grocery store, Adam was filling up two grocery carts with cases of Dr Pepper?

What's he going to *do* with all that Dr Pepper? Eve wondered. Who's going to drink it?

"So starving people really go for this Dr Pepper stuff, huh?" she asked suspiciously.

Adam blinked and looked away. "Yeah," he said.

No way, Eve thought. You're lying.

She opened her mouth to ask him another

question, but just then he dashed off. She caught up to him in front of a huge display of pipe tobacco. "Hey! I'm going to need *all* of this!" he announced.

Eve closed her eyes.

Oh, man. This was nuts. Totally loony. Why would poor people want pipe tobacco?

"Run, Eve, run," she mumbled.

But she couldn't leave him. He was just too pathetic.

Besides, he was paying her a *lot* of money!

It took the rest of the afternoon to finish the dry goods on Adam's list. Dozens of bags of flour, sugar, and rice—all in fifty-pound bags. Cases and cases of toilet paper. Tissues. Paper towels. Cartons and cartons of powdered milk.

They had to rent a self-storage unit just to hold all the stuff, because it was too much to fit into the U-Haul truck at once.

"We'll have to rent a refrigerated truck tomorrow for the beef and poultry," Adam said as he padlocked the storage unit.

"It's your life," Eve said matter-of-factly. "And, in case you were wondering, it's a dandy."

"I guess we'll need another storage locker," Adam noted.

"No problem," Eve said. She reached into her bag, where she was now carrying part of the baseball card collection. "We'll have Whitey Ford and

Warren Spahn take care of it."

"You know, Eve," Adam began in an awkward tone of voice. "Don't get mad, okay? But I'd just be lost without you."

His eyes were as soft and innocent and pleading as a puppy's. But Eve knew he was falling in love.

With *her*.

Yikes.

No way, she thought. She didn't want this poor fool falling all over himself for her. Even if he was just a nerdy jerk, he was kind of sweet at the same time. Sweet and cute.

She didn't want to hurt him.

"Did you hear me?" Adam asked. "Really—I'd be lost without you."

"Thank you," she said without a single note of encouragement in her voice.

"And, um...," Adam went on. "I guess...I guess you and I, uh..."

"Don't even think about it," Eve said bluntly. She wanted to make herself perfectly clear. There was no chance for him. None. End of topic. Forget it.

"I'm sorry," she went on. "That sounds mean, but believe me, it would be meaner if I *didn't* say it. Okay?"

Adam swallowed hard. "Okay."

Eve could see him struggling with his feelings.

"Now, let's take the truck back and get something to eat," she suggested cheerfully. She hopped up behind the wheel.

Adam followed her quietly. She caught a glimpse of his dejected face.

Stop feeling sorry for him! You did him a favor, she reminded herself.

But he still looked kind of like a puppy. A hurt puppy now.

As Eve pulled onto the highway, Adam cleared his throat.

Okay, he thought. If he couldn't have Eve...well, okay. Then he couldn't.

But he wasn't going to give up on having a wife. That was one of the most important things he'd come to the surface to find.

"There's something else I would like you to help me with," he began. The importance of the whole thing made him hesitate. He didn't want to get his feelings hurt again.

"Name it," Eve said.

"Well, this is going to sound a little crazy," Adam warned her.

"Oh, I'm sure it will!" she said, laughing already. "But what is it? Anything for starving people."

"This isn't for starving people," Adam said. "This is for me."

"Think of me as your genie," Eve said. "Just ask."

"Well..." He stalled, reluctant to spit it out. "Okay. I would like you to help me find a wife."

"A *wife*?" She sounded as if she couldn't quite believe her ears.

"Yes," Adam said solemnly.

"What for?" Eve asked.

"Because I want to get married," Adam said.

"*Why*?"

Isn't it obvious? he thought. "Because I don't want to be alone."

"You can be single and not alone," Eve said as if she thought that was the most obvious thing in the world. "Marriage stinks."

"It does?" Adam felt a little shocked.

But then he began to wonder. Maybe she was right. After all, *she'd* been living on the surface all these years. He hadn't.

"Sure. Everybody knows that," Eve announced. "Ask my divorced sisters. Or ask my divorced mom and dad."

"They're *all* divorced?" Now Adam was truly shocked.

"*Everybody's* divorced," Eve stated flatly.

"It didn't used to be that way," Adam mumbled, trying to take it in.

"I wouldn't know," Eve said, steering the truck into the exit lane of the freeway.

Adam sat quietly for a moment. Then he sneaked a glance at Eve.

She seemed to be thinking about something.

"What kind of wife are you looking for?" she asked after a few seconds.

"One who's not a mutant," Adam stated.

She laughed. "No dogs, huh? Okay."

"And, if possible, I'd like to marry someone from *Pasadena*," Adam added.

Eve shot him another glance. "Are you kidding?" she muttered. Then she shook her head. "No. Nothing you say is ever a joke, is it?"

Not usually, Adam thought. Although his father had told him some pretty good jokes a long time ago.

"Okay," Eve said. "When do you need her by? This...wife."

"Two weeks," Adam answered.

"Well, I could probably get you a date in two weeks," Eve said. "But to locate a nonmutant from Pasadena? Who wants to marry *you*?" She grinned. "*That* could take time."

"That's what I was afraid of," Adam admitted.

That's the one thing he didn't have—time.

A horrible thought crossed his mind. What if he had to go back to the shelter for the next few years—without a wife?

What would he do then?

chapter seven

Later that day, they sat in a coffee shop, having a quick bite to eat.

A wife for Adam, Eve thought. That *was* going to be a challenge. Did she know *anyone* who would fall for this guy?

No. Not the way he was now anyway.

Did she know anyone she would even *wish* this guy on?

No.

Well...

No.

This was going to take some thought, Eve decided. Some focused, carefully considered thought.

And some advice from Troy, her roommate.

"We'd better get back to work," Adam said. He got to his feet.

"Here." Eve held out her car keys. "You drive."

"Uh, I've never driven before," Adam said, sounding reluctant. "I don't know how."

"Come on," Eve said, pushing the keys into his hand. "It's easy. You'll learn."

Ten nightmarish minutes later, Adam fishtailed around the corner onto the street where Eve lived. The tires on her car locked and squealed, the brakes screamed, and the car lurched forward way too fast for the quiet residential neighborhood.

Finally they landed in a semi-parked position— half in the street and half up on the curb.

Eve knew her face was white, drained of blood.

"Get out!" she screamed at the top of her lungs.

"The engine is still running," Adam reported, pointing at the key.

Eve ripped the key out of the ignition. "Now, get out!"

"Yes, ma'am!" Adam obeyed.

"And stop that ma'am stuff!" Eve screamed.

"Sorry!" Adam apologized back.

Eve climbed out of the car, shaking. She was grateful to feel her feet back on solid, unmoving ground.

What could she have possibly been thinking

when she allowed this...this...*maniac* to drive?

"You almost got us killed!" she screamed.

"I told you I've never driven before!" Adam shouted.

"Never drive again!" Eve advised him.

"You said it would be easy!" Adam argued.

"I was wrong!"

The two of them stared at each other for a moment, both still shaking from the experience.

Then Adam's gaze moved to the small bungalow behind her.

"Is this your house?" he asked.

"Yes!" Eve yelled. It was as if she were stuck in yelling gear—and couldn't get out of it.

"I like it." Adam smiled at her with that puppy-love grin.

Ugh! she thought, wincing.

Eve tossed Adam his cigar box full of baseball cards and stormed off toward her house.

"And next time you see a sign that says one way—read it!" she yelled over her shoulder.

Then she caught sight of a guy, fabulous-looking and well-built, coming out the front door of her house. Cliff—her ex-boyfriend. He was wearing a T-shirt and exercise shorts. And he was carrying a carton of clothes.

"What are you complaining about now?" Cliff asked as he bounded down the steps toward Adam and Eve.

Eve glared at her ex-boyfriend. Why, *why* isn't he gone yet? she wondered. What is this? My lucky day?

"What are you doing here?" she asked him, not answering his question.

"I forgot some of my stuff," Cliff said.

"*Your* stuff? Let me see that." She started plowing through the box.

Yeah, okay, she realized. It *was* Cliff's stuff. Cliff, the latest guy with the legs, body, and hair that she really, really liked—but who was so shallow that if he'd been a puddle, you'd barely be able to see a reflection in him.

She pulled a pair of old briefs out of the box and held them up.

"You came back for *these*?" Eve asked, amazed.

"Hey, they're Ralph Laurens," Cliff answered. Then he turned his attention to Adam. "And who is this interesting-looking guy?"

Eve gritted her teeth. Was Cliff going to be a jerk to Adam?

"This is Adam," she said in a neutral voice. "Adam, meet Cliff."

Adam held out his hand to shake. "How do you do?" he said.

"I do fine, Adam. How about yourself?" Cliff asked. He glanced at Eve. She could read on his face that he was wondering just what was going on between her and Adam.

Well, let him wonder.

"Go home, Cliff," Eve said wearily. "Wherever that might be."

Cliff ambled down the walk, smiling. When he was gone, Adam turned politely to Eve. "May I ask you a question?" he began.

"Former boyfriend," Eve answered. "And yes, I'll admit it. I've still kind of got a thing for him. That's what you wanted to know, isn't it?"

"Actually, no," Adam replied. "Cliff said he came back for underwear that was Ralph Lauren's." He paused. "I guess I was just wondering why Cliff likes to wear another man's underpants."

Whoa! Eve thought.

Would this guy ever stop blowing her mind with how naïve he was?

On the other hand, judging by his clothes, it *was* pretty obvious that he'd never heard of Ralph Lauren before.

Never mind, she told herself. Who cares how idiotic he is? He's paying me a lot of money. A thousand a week.

Just keep focused on that, she reminded herself.

It was a job. Not a great job, maybe, but not that bad either. In fact, all the shopping was sort of fun.

Eve led Adam into the house and introduced him to Troy. She hid a smile at the way Adam's eyes widened when he took in Troy's triple ear-rings and peroxide-blond hair.

"Ooo-la-la!" Troy cried, looking Adam up and down. "Honey, this one's *too* fabulous!"

"Uh…thank you." Adam looked confused.

Eve turned a laugh into a cough. "I'm going to take a shower," she announced. "You two hang out. Get to know each other."

And she hurried off to the bathroom before either of them could say anything.

After her shower, she and Troy escaped to the kitchen to talk about Adam.

"Well, what do you think?" she asked Troy as the two of them chopped vegetables.

Troy carefully arranged a few pieces of sushi on a platter and leaned closer to Eve.

"This guy is un-be-*liev*-able!" he whispered.

Eve grinned.

"I knew you'd like him," she said.

"Darlin', this is *X-Files* stuff! Think about it!" Troy waved a hand in the air. "The guy's got all this easily negotiable property—right? Could be diamonds as easily as baseball cards. And he's obviously setting something up very big. Like a self-sustaining island off the coast of South America, for instance. Or perhaps he's the head of a cult that's doing illegal things with poultry and pipe tobacco. Whatever it is, it's weird. And secret. Totally top secret."

Eve squinted, thinking about it.

Maybe Troy was right. All the stuff Adam was collecting was weird, that was for sure. Totally weird. And his story—about the food being for homeless people. It didn't add up.

Her stomach muscles clenched. I hope it's *not* something illegal, she thought. I don't need that kind of trouble.

"Wow! Come quick! Have you heard this?" Adam called from the living room.

Eve raced inside. What now? she wondered.

Adam was staring at the stereo speakers, entranced.

"The vocals come out of one speaker, and the instrumentals come out of the other one!" he announced, his eyes wide.

Stereo? He's impressed with stereo sound?

Eve flipped her hand at him. "Whatever floats your boat," she said. She went back into the kitchen and fetched a tray of drinks to go with the appetizers Troy was making.

A moment later, Troy carried the platter of fresh sea urchin wrapped in seaweed into the living room.

"Here you go," Eve said, handing Adam a glass of club soda.

"Thank-Q!" Adam said.

Ugh! Did he *have* to talk like that?

"So, Adam, where on earth are you from?"

Troy raised his eyebrows, waiting for the answer.

"Out of town," Eve answered. "That's all he'll say."

"It's a very small place," Adam said. "People don't even know it's there."

"And it's called...?" Troy waited.

"Maybe Eve can guess," Adam suggested. "She's psychic."

"Really? Since *when*?" Troy asked sarcastically.

"Since that guy rear-ended me in Palm Springs, okay?" Eve shot back defensively. She gave Troy a cut-me-a-break glare.

"Oh. Yeah. Right." Troy rolled his eyes.

"I even guessed his hotel, didn't I?" She waited for Adam to back her up.

"Right on the button." Adam beamed at her.

Adam stared at Eve. She was by far the most wonderful, amazing person who had ever walked the earth. What could he possibly do or say to change her mind and make her like him better? Make her fall in love with him?

And if he *couldn't* do that, then what could he do to make sure that the wife he found was as beautiful, interesting, funny, and *alive* as Eve was?

Everything about her was perfect. Enchanting. Wonderful.

Take her laugh, for instance. It was quick and sharp and maybe even a little bit biting—but it was filled with so much energy and enthusiasm. How could you mind when someone laughed at you when their laugh was so musical? Adam thought.

Or take the way she flipped her hair onto her shoulder. It could seem like she did it to show people how attractive she was. But really, Adam knew Eve's hair was like a security blanket to her. Flipping it onto her shoulder made her feel protected.

Adam thought even the way she rolled her eyes when he didn't understand things was adorable.

Because, behind her impatient eyes, he saw that she was really a very kind person. Very honest. Very real.

He let out a sigh and gazed at her across the coffee table, not even trying to hide the way he felt.

Eve caught his expression and rolled her eyes. Again.

See? Adorable, Adam thought. Completely adorable.

Troy hardly seemed to notice. He was still trying to find out where Adam came from.

"Well, then, Miss Psychic," Troy went on, challenging Eve, "guess his hometown."

"Give me your hand," Eve instructed Adam.

Adam gladly held out his hand for Eve, and she began rubbing her finger slowly, gently, around the surface of his palm.

Slowly. Around and around.

Oh, my, Adam thought. He felt his heartbeat pick up and his skin begin to get warm all over. The feel of her soft index finger. The way her other hand felt, touching the back of his hand. Cradling it.

He'd never had physical contact with a woman. Other than his mother. And he had never felt *anything* as amazing as this.

"Okay," Eve began. "Let's see..."

She stared at his palm. Adam began to breathe a little more heavily than usual.

"You okay?" she asked him.

"Um-hum," he managed to get out.

"Okay." She went back to his palm. "I'm seeing...snow. Lots and lots of snow. Way up north. Are we getting hot?"

"Yes. Definitely," Adam said absently.

"You live in...Alaska," Eve guessed. "I mean, I figure you must live *somewhere* pretty remote, because you definitely act like you've never been in normal civilization before. And I'd say the only way in or out of your place is by plane and...this part's not completely clear...but you've come down here for food and supplies and...to find a wife!"

With that, she tossed his hand back in his lap triumphantly. As if she knew she was right.

Adam just smiled. She was *so* wonderful.

"That's right?" Troy asked, astonished that Adam wasn't denying it.

Adam didn't answer. He just stared at Eve. "I've never met anyone like you in my life," he said.

"She's *right*?" Troy demanded, even more unbelieving.

"Hey, jerkface! I have this thing," Eve insisted.

"I've got goose bumps all over me," Adam admitted.

"See?" Eve glared at Troy.

But Troy still wasn't buying it.

"Let me just ask you a few questions," he went on, grilling Adam. "If you're from Alaska, when did it become a state?"

That's easy, Adam thought. His father had taught him *all* about American History when he was growing up in the shelter. Every last detail.

"Nineteen fifty-nine," Adam answered.

"Who used to own it?" Troy quizzed.

"Russia."

"When did we get it from them?"

"Eighteen sixty-seven," Adam replied. "In a deal called Seward's Folly."

This was fun, Adam thought. He knew so much about Alaska, it was easy to fool Troy into thinking he was from there.

"What's the capital?" Troy demanded.

"Juneau," Adam replied.

Troy practically jumped up from the couch. "Hel-lo! It's Anchorage! Gotcha!" he cried.

"Sorry," Adam smiled at Troy. "That's the largest city, but it's not the capital."

Troy hurried out of the room without saying another word.

"Where's he going?" Adam asked, alone now with Eve.

"He's checking your answers on his computer," she explained.

Adam's eyes lit up. "He has a *computer*?"

"Sure."

"In the *house*?"

"No. We keep it in the backyard. Of *course* it's in the house. It's in his bedroom."

Wow, Adam thought. This was too much. Of all the things he'd seen so far, a computer was the one that would most impress and amaze his father. Calvin had been a scientist and inventor before they went into the bomb shelter. He loved technical stuff like that.

Adam had to get a look at this computer himself—if Eve didn't mind.

"May I please be excused?" Adam asked.

"Uh...yeah," she said, although she looked surprised at the question.

Adam leaped up and found his way to Troy's bedroom. Troy was sitting in the dimly lit room, a map of Alaska on his computer screen. The colorful pictures on the screen kept changing as he pushed a button on some kind of little object that rolled around on the desk.

Adam stared at it from the doorway for a moment, but couldn't resist getting a closer look. Slowly, he walked up and stood behind Troy's back.

"This must be very new," Adam said, transfixed by the technological wonder. He remembered what his father had told him about the first computers ever made. They completely filled large rooms—and all they could do was compute basic math problems.

"Yeah," Troy muttered. "I only got this one a few months ago."

"It's so small," Adam commented.

"Yeah. But it's got thirty-two megs of RAM and a one-gig hard drive. You a hacker?"

"I don't think so," Adam said, not entirely sure.

"Well, you're right," Troy admitted. "Juneau is the capital of Alaska." Then he quickly covered the screen with his hand. "What's the highest peak?" he asked Adam.

"Mount McKinley," Adam answered quickly. "It's also the highest point in North America."

"Okay," Troy said, giving in. "Maybe she *is* psychic!" He stood up. "Come on. Let's eat."

After dinner, the three of them sat around the

dining table, trying to figure out how Eve could help Adam find a wife.

"Well, first we have to start with the clothes," Troy decided.

Eve shot Adam a glance. "You understand that, don't you? That you have no chance of meeting a woman dressed like that."

"All right." Adam was willing to accept her word for it. After all, she seemed to know everything about everything—especially when it came to dealing with people.

That's one of the things that he was so crazy about, he realized. The fact that Eve seemed to understand people. She had a real gift for figuring out what was going on.

"So," Eve said, turning back to Troy. "What are you seeing, fashion-wise?"

Troy eyed Adam up and down.

"I don't know..." Troy hesitated. "This is tough—given the...raw material."

"Money is no object," Eve reminded him.

"How about Maxfield's?" Troy suggested.

"Naw, he's too conservative for that," Eve said. "Ralph Lauren?"

Eve nodded. "Okay, for casual. But what about Tommy Hilfiger?"

"Could be," Troy agreed. "But, you know, if he's got the money, there's no beating Armani."

"True," Eve said. She turned to Adam. "What

do you think?" she asked him.

Adam didn't care. All he knew was that he was having an amazing time on the surface. He felt as if his life had just begun. As if he hadn't actually been alive before, and now he was starting a whole new existence. Surface existence.

He also knew he wanted to do whatever it took—anything Eve recommended—so he could begin his new existence with the right person.

With a wife.

Maybe even with Eve.

After all, if he did what she told him to, maybe she'd change her mind about him. Right? Maybe she could turn him into someone she'd like. Someone attractive.

"Whatever you two think," Adam replied. He stared deeply into Eve's eyes. Eyes that were bluer than blue. "Whatever you want. I'll go along with anything. Anything!"

chapter eight

"Where are we going?" Adam asked from the backseat of Eve's car as they sped along the high-way.

"Rodeo Drive," Troy answered. "When it comes down to it, there's nowhere else to start on a major shopping expedition. We're hitting Brynne's."

"What's Brynne's?" Adam asked.

"Only the newest, hippest store in L.A.," Troy explained. "So when we get there, act snotty."

Act snotty? Adam thought. Why?

It's going to be a *very* long time before I understand surface people, he decided.

After that, Adam rode quietly in the backseat,

his back straight and his posture perfect.

Troy slumped in the front passenger seat, sprawled on the armrests. As much as it was possible to sprawl in Eve's little car.

"Isn't it a little tiring to sit up straight like that all the time?" Eve asked, glancing at Adam in the rearview mirror.

"No." Adam didn't really understand the question. His parents had taught him to sit up straight and he'd done it all his life.

"Really? You don't get tired of it?" Troy asked.

"It's fine," Adam replied. "Just give it a try."

Eve and Troy sat up straighter, and Adam laughed. They looked totally uncomfortable.

"Come on." Eve laughed. She parked the car and hopped out. "It's clothing time!"

As soon as Adam stepped into Brynne's, he felt a rush of excitement. The store was beautiful! Dark maple cabinets lined all the walls. And the place even smelled good, somehow.

But mostly Adam was excited about getting a new look. Some new clothes. Clothes that would help him fit in with all these interesting people on the surface.

Clothes that someone like Eve wouldn't make fun of.

He tried on a black Armani suit with a blue dress shirt and silver tie. He cautiously stepped out of the dressing room.

Eve's eyes lit up.

All right! Adam thought. She looks happy. I must be doing *something* right!

"Yeah," Eve told the salesclerks. "That's good. Now how about that putty-gray suit? And shirts to go with. And some casual-dressy clothes too."

"Silk T-shirts," Troy suggested. "And linen pants. And belts. We need *accessories*!" he called.

"I can't believe how great you look," Eve said to Adam. "How beautifully the clothes fit you— right off the rack."

She stared at him with a new look in her eyes. A look that made Adam's face feel warm.

"Anyway," Eve went on. "Now you're date material. With a wardrobe like this, you'll be able to meet and pick up women pretty easily."

Troy chimed in, "Even *I'm* impressed."

"You *must* rush all the alterations," Eve told the sales staff. "Mr. Webber leaves for New Delhi tomorrow morning."

Adam laughed. She was acting as if she and Troy were assistants to an important businessman or something.

He watched the salesclerk rush around, trying to make sure that everything was arranged.

"We certainly want to keep our customers happy," the clerk said cheerfully.

After Brynne's, Eve drove them to her favorite sports and sports-clothing store to get Adam some stuff he could wear just hanging around.

Biking shorts. Jogging shoes. Sandals. More T-shirts.

Boy, oh, boy, Adam thought. He felt tired from trying on so many different outfits. Buying a whole new wardrobe is—

Wait a minute. Something caught his eye.

What *were* those things? Skates? With the wheels all lined up in a row?

Adam was an ace roller skater. He'd skated all his life, racing around and around, through the cavernous space in his parents' bomb shelter. In his father's old skates, of course.

But he'd never seen anything like *these*.

Adam dropped the sweat pants he was holding and hurried across the room.

"What are they?" he asked, picking up the skates and staring at the strange configuration. Four wheels in a row!

"In-line skates," Eve answered with a shrug.

"May I please try them on right now?" Adam asked urgently.

"Sure!" a salesman said. He helped Adam into a pair of the nicest skates in the store.

Wow, Adam thought. I've got to buy them. And then try them out—today!

Forty minutes later, Adam, Eve, and Troy pulled up to the parking lot at Venice Beach—a long park with flat walkways.

Nice choice, Adam thought. This was clearly a perfect place to skate.

He hopped out of the car, his in-line skates already clamped on tight.

"Hey, wait!" Eve called. But Adam couldn't help himself. He instantly skated off like a pro, leaving them behind.

He zoomed ahead, then circled back, doing a spectacular spin or two—not to show off, but just to try out the new equipment on his feet.

Wow. These in-line things were great! You could go so much faster than on roller skates.

But, really, the best part was being able to skate outside. In the sunlight! Under the magnificent blue sky!

It was heaven, Adam thought.

Then he began to take in the other people who were skating, too. So many other people. Especially women. Beautiful women dressed in tight sports tops with their midriffs bare...

Adam gulped.

And skintight shorts out of some kind of stretchy material that was shiny and colorful...

And...*whoa*!

Two gorgeous young women walked toward Adam. Both were wearing what looked to him like underwear—teeny bras and teeny-tiny underpants. Tied together at the sides with strings.

One woman's outfit was electric blue. The

other wore bright red.

The sight of the gorgeous nearly naked bodies made him dizzy. All at once, the sky began to spin....

He tried to swing around, to watch them pass by, but his feet flew out from under him on the turn and...

Whoa! He hit the pavement in a horrendous crash.

Eve and Troy skated up. Eve bent over him, worried.

"Are you all right?" she asked nervously.

"That was a totally amazing crash!" Troy remarked.

"You should see him drive!" Eve said sarcastically. But she bent even closer to Adam. "Hey! Are you okay?" she asked, sounding worried.

Am I all right? Adam wondered, his head sort of spinning from the fall.

Yes. Except...

Except...

He wanted to say something. To speak to Eve. To tell her he was all right. But he couldn't concentrate on her just then. There was something behind her. Something amazing!

He sat up and stared at it. Silently.

"He's got a concussion," Troy declared.

"You think?" Eve asked.

"Well, look at him!" Troy answered. "He's

completely out of it!"

Adam wasn't listening. He stood up and began walking.

Toward the *ocean*!

It was hard walking in the sand with his skates on. But Adam hardly noticed. All he could see was the vast, amazingly blue ocean stretching out in front of him.

The waves crested and broke, crested and broke, on the sand.

He took a deep breath in, loving the smell of salt in the air.

Finally, as he neared the water, Adam sat down in the sand to take off his skates. Then he jumped up and made a running, yelling dive into the water.

"That water's freezing!" Eve remarked, watching from fifty feet away.

"He's from *Alaska*, remember?" Troy shot back.

Adam dove under, then popped up through the surface of the water.

Yes! He threw his fists in the air. He felt as if he might burst with pure joy.

"*I love this*!" he shouted.

Eve and Troy watched the whole scene from the back of the beach.

Adam just didn't make sense, Eve thought.

He didn't add up.

Here was this guy who collected baseball cards—but didn't know how much they were worth.

He wanted hundreds of pounds of frozen meat—but wouldn't say who it was for.

He'd never driven a car—but could skate circles around half the show-offs in Venice Beach.

He dressed like a nerd—but looked fantastic when you changed his clothes. Who knew he had such a great body? And such incredible green eyes?

And he acted like a lunatic about stuff that only kids got excited about. Like seeing the ocean.

"I'm getting a little scared," Troy said softly. "How about you?"

Yeah, Eve thought. More than a little.

Because it looked as if she had volunteered to help out a total nutcase.

chapter nine

"So this is it. This is your big night," Troy said to Adam. The three of them pulled up at The Forties, a hip nightclub in a chic section of L.A.

Right, Adam thought as he stepped out of Eve's small, dirty Ford Geo and straightened his tie. My big night. The night I finally get to meet women.

And maybe...if I'm lucky...find a wife.

He glanced at Eve. One glance made his heart race with excitement.

She looked fantastic. Her shimmery black dress with thin straps made her shoulders look amazingly smooth. Her hair moved and glistened. He loved looking at the way it draped on the back of her neck.

Plus she smelled *wonderful*, Adam thought.

What was that smell, anyway? Fruits and flowers all mixed up together? He'd never smelled anything like that.

His stomach did a flip when he let himself watch her that way. And he knew what that meant. It meant his feelings were all mixed up inside. His feelings about finding a wife.

Get a grip, he told himself. Quit staring at her. This is your chance to meet women and find someone you can spend the rest of your life with.

But part of him knew that he'd already found that someone. Eve.

He shook his head. He had to put those thoughts out of his mind. She didn't feel that way about him. She'd made that totally clear, hadn't she?

"You ready?" Troy called.

Adam tore his eyes away from Eve.

"Yes. Ready," he answered. He headed for the club.

As they reached the front door, Troy started to lead the way inside. But Adam quickly grabbed his arm and pulled him back.

"What?" Troy snapped, annoyed.

"Ladies first, Troy!" Adam reminded him, slightly horrified that Troy could make such a huge etiquette mistake. "Boy, that was close!"

Troy rolled his eyes, but stepped aside so that

Eve could enter before them. Then the two guys followed her into the dark club. The three of them looked around.

What a fabulous place, Adam thought. It was very glamorous and very dark. It was decorated like the 1940s nightclubs he'd seen pictured in old magazines. Small, round tables lit with individual chrome lamps surrounded a central dance floor.

The dance floor was crowded with people who were all dressed up for a night on the town.

Adam felt his heart race again. He scanned the room, gazing at the women. Wow. Most of them were wearing short, low-cut dresses.

The music was wonderful too, Adam realized. Just the kind of thing he loved. Mostly it was big band and swing music from the 40s. His favorite. His mom had taught him to dance during all those years in the shelter.

"My goodness gracious! This place is *something*!" Adam exclaimed.

"Look unimpressed," Eve instructed him.

"Bored, even," Troy added.

Bored? Adam thought. Why?

He tried to follow their instructions, although he wasn't sure why he was doing it. He wasn't bored, that was for sure. This was incredible!

But he had vowed to do whatever Eve told him to do. He was smart enough to know that he needed help—from someone who knew how the world really worked. Today. In the 1990s.

Okay, he thought. Bored.

He made his face go dead and pretended he was watching an episode of *The Honeymooners* for the two hundredth time.

"No. *Vaguely* bored," Troy said, trying to correct him.

Adam tried again.

"No. Act unimpressed, but still interested," Eve urged.

Adam twisted his face into another expression.

"No! Not crazy!" Eve hissed.

"Do I really look crazy?" Adam asked.

"Yes!"

"Be loose," Troy suggested.

Adam let his muscles slump and leaned against a wall next to another woman, smiling at her as if they were best friends.

Eve closed her eyes for a minute.

"No. This isn't working," she said. "Tell you what, Adam. Just be yourself."

"Thank-Q," Adam said, feeling instantly relieved.

"Wow. Good advice," Troy said to Eve. "He looks more relaxed than anyone in the place."

"On him it works," Eve agreed, nodding. "But I wouldn't recommend it to normal humans."

Eve scanned the room, checking out the crowd.

"Yeah—there are a lot of women I know here

tonight," she told Adam. "But maybe the best way to get you loosened up is to introduce you to a few *guys* first. Let you get your feet wet. Talking to strangers. Then, when you've had some practice, you can plunge into the dating thing."

"All right, I guess," Adam was about to say. But Eve wasn't waiting for him to okay her plan. She was already walking off toward two guys who were standing near the bar.

The guys waved when they saw Eve and Troy approaching.

"Jason, Jonathan, this is Adam!" Eve shouted to be heard above the music. "Adam, that's them," she said.

Quickly he held out his hand to shake.

"How do you do? It's very nice to meet you, Jason and Jonathan," Adam said. Then he leaned in closer, to share his own little secret. "My mother always told me that if you meet a person for the first time, it's easier to remember their names if you use those names right away."

Jason and Jonathan just stared at Adam.

"He's from Alaska," Troy offered.

"Ohhhh." Both guys nodded.

Behind Eve, Adam noticed another woman approaching them. A beautiful woman with an amazing body, wearing a very sexy dress.

The woman staggered a little. She came up and tapped Eve on the shoulder.

Eve turned around and scowled, looking less than overjoyed.

"Sophie," Eve muttered.

"Hi, there, Eve. Who's the hunk?" Sophie slurred.

"Get lost, Sophie," Eve snapped.

Why? Adam wondered. Why should she get lost? I thought we came here to meet women. To find me a wife.

Sophie ignored Eve and pushed her way up to Adam.

"Hi. I'm Sophie," she purred, tilting her head up into Adam's face.

Her voice made Adam feel slightly warm. He smiled and said, "Hello, Sophie, I'm Adam Webber."

"Adam lives in Alaska," Jason offered, sort of like a warning.

"Wow," Sophie said, taking a step back.

Oh, brother, Adam thought. Why did they have to mention Alaska? It's not even true that I live in Alaska. And most people don't want to go live there because it's so empty and far away— and cold.

Maybe I should say something to let her know that I'm interested in other parts of the world, he thought.

Maybe something in French.

"*Ça va bien en Alaska,*" Adam said. In French,

that meant: things are pretty good where I come from.

"You speak beautiful French!" Sophie shot back. Then, with a halfway decent accent herself, she said, "*J'ai habité Paris pendant une année.*"

Adam smiled. Sophie was nice, he thought. Nice—and beautiful. It was sweet of her to answer him in French.

Maybe he would be able to find a woman—other than Eve—whom he could fall in love with after all.

No way, Eve thought. Not Sophie and Adam. No way.

This was *not* a match made in heaven.

For one thing, Sophie wasn't good enough for Adam. Not by a long shot.

And once Sophie found out about his money? She'd be all over him, and he'd never have a chance at finding the right wife. The one who could bring him...whatever he wanted. Like true happiness or something.

Eve stepped between them and took Adam by the hand. Then she dragged him away from Sophie.

"Quit showing off!" she scolded Adam. "We're here on business."

"Good-bye," Adam called longingly over his shoulder as he followed Eve away.

"Not good-bye," Sophie called. "*Au revoir.* Until we meet again."

Adam let Eve lead him to a table.

"What are you doing? I thought I was here to meet women," he complained. "Right?"

"Not that one!" Eve said.

"I like her."

"I know. But don't be so obvious!" Eve scolded.

She plopped down at their table and sipped her drink. Then she and Troy began scoping out women in the club. Trying to find someone for Adam.

Except that none of them seemed right to Eve.

Half the women there were too beautiful—and knew it. They wouldn't give Adam the time of day. The other half were just—the wrong kind.

"What about *her*?" Adam asked as a leggy blonde strutted in front of their table.

Eve shook her head.

"No. Not your type."

Adam sighed and leaned back in his chair.

"Well, what about *her*?" he asked, nodding toward a woman in high, high heels and a dress about four sizes too small.

Eve shook her head again.

No way, she thought. Adam deserved someone nicer than that. That woman was just there to pick up men—and dip into their wallets.

"How about *her*?" Now Adam sounded

annoyed. He nodded toward a brunette with pouty lips and a too-cool-for-you expression on her face.

"No way," Eve said.

"Why?" Adam demanded. "I think she's very attractive!"

"Adam, no. Look at her hair. Her fingernails. Her make up. She's a viper. She's got trouble written all over her," Eve said. "She's not for you."

Adam frowned, but he didn't argue.

"Just wait," Eve counseled him. "Don't be so impatient."

The place was so packed, all they had to do was wait a moment, and another stunning girl was bound to come walking past, Eve reasoned.

"How about this one?" Adam asked as a supermodel blonde edged past their table.

"Are you kidding? You wouldn't even be a crumb on her table!" Eve snapped. "You don't see that?"

"Eve!" Troy shot her a glance that she read instantly: He thought she was being unnecessarily cruel.

"Well, I'm trying to educate him," Eve defended herself. "It's nothing personal."

"Adam, I think for you, we should go for 'sweet,'" Troy suggested, trying to soften the blow.

"Okay," Adam agreed happily.

"Yeah, sweet!" Eve chimed in. "That's a nice

way of putting it."

"What do I say to Miss Sweet when I meet her?" Adam asked Troy.

"You got *me*!" Troy said. "Eve?"

"It's not so much what you say but how you say it," Eve advised. "Women like men who are unpredictable. Basically, they want someone they think they can't have. Same with guys. That's why everybody is walking around here sending off you-can't-have-me signals."

"That's ridiculous," Adam said.

"Maybe. But that's how it works," Eve insisted.

Troy leaned toward Adam and pointed out a redhead at the hors d'oeuvres table. She had a sweet face, as ordered. And her very short satin slip-dress didn't conceal her long legs at all.

"There's Miss Sweet now," Troy said, nodding toward the young woman.

"Yeah," Eve agreed. "Could be. Go say hello, Adam."

"And then what? After hello?"

"Say something *surprising* and *funny*," Eve advised. "Lie, if necessary."

"Okay," Adam said, standing up. "Surprising and funny. I've got just the ticket for that. I know a joke my father used to tell about a duck who bought some lip balm...."

Eve shook her head, but moved a bit closer so she could eavesdrop as Adam headed for the hors d'oeurves table. He cleared his throat.

"Hi," he said bravely.

"Yes?"

The cold stare from Miss Sweet was more on the sour side.

"Uh, I was wondering if you might help me," Adam said. "I...I seem to have lost my Congressional Medal of Honor somewhere around here."

Oh, brother, Eve thought. How pathetic!

The redhead stared at him for a moment or two, blankly. Then, amazingly, she laughed.

"Oh, now, *that's* a great one," she said, giving him a little applause.

A huge smile spread across Adam's face. He looked so proud of himself, Eve thought.

"You like it?" he asked.

"Yeah," the redhead said. "Bravo. I do."

Weird, Eve thought. He gets away with things that no one else would get away with!

Just then, another woman walked up. She stood beside Adam and glanced at the redhead. It was as if she wanted to be introduced. Obviously, the two were friends.

"This is my new friend," Miss Sweet began, waiting for Adam to fill in his name.

"Adam Webber."

"He's really funny!" Miss Sweet told her friend.

"Hi," the friend said. "I'm Heather!"

Adam stared into her eyes, which were green and almond-shaped. "Heather," he said. "I don't believe I've ever heard that name before."

Never heard the name *Heather*? He's got to be kidding, right? Eve thought.

Or maybe not.

Both girls decided that it was another joke. They laughed.

"Yeah, right," Heather said.

"I told you! He's funny!" the redhead said, yelling to be heard above the music.

Eve watched with her mouth hanging open. She couldn't believe it. Adam was hitting it off with two gorgeous women. In fact, in another two minutes they were hanging all over him!

"We're both professional dancers," Miss Sweet told Adam, glancing toward the dance floor.

"Really?" Adam asked.

"Yeah. You dance?" Heather sounded ready and willing.

"I took a dance lesson every day of my life until just recently," Adam answered.

"You're kidding!" Miss Sweet said.

"Nope. My mother taught me," Adam explained.

Heather and Miss Sweet exchanged uncertain glances. Eve knew what they were thinking.

Was this guy for real? Was it a joke? It was kind-of hard to tell.

"Okay," Miss Sweet said. "Let's give it a try."

The two of them moved toward the dance floor as a hip swing tune began to play. Adam held out his arms in waltz position. But Miss Sweet took his hands and led him into some late '90s moves.

Eve watched nervously. At first, Adam didn't quite seem to know what to do—but pretty soon they were tearing up the place.

Eve took one look at what was going on and hurried to the bar. She needed *information*!

"Jason! Jonathan! What do you know about the redhead with the guy from Alaska and the woman up there talking to the DJ?" she shouted.

Jason shrugged. "Don't know them," he shouted back. "You?"

Jonathan shook his head. "Let me ask Blair and Boyer!" he called, pushing to get through the crowd at the bar.

Eve nodded, then craned her neck to get a better view of what was happening on the dance floor.

By then, Heather had cut in on Adam and Miss Sweet. Now Heather and Adam were dancing so well together that everyone else on the floor had stopped just to watch.

Eve stalked back to her table and sat down across from Troy. She felt her face growing hot. She didn't know why, but for some stupid reason, all of a sudden she felt—jealous.

What did Adam think she was, anyway? Did he

think it was her life's work to haul him all over L.A. to meet beautiful women? That he could spend the night showing off? Dancing? And not even spend a minute dancing with *her*?

"You know, he's pretty good," Troy muttered.

"Shut up!" Eve snapped, rising from her chair.

Just as the dance ended, Eve put two fingers between her lips and let loose with a sharp, shrill whistle. Like a guy calling his dog.

"Must you?" Troy asked, embarrassed.

Eve ignored him. As soon as the whistle caught Adam's attention, she pointed to him, then motioned for him to get his butt back over to the table. Right now!

"What in the world is wrong with you?" Troy yelled at her.

Good question, Eve thought. What *is* wrong with me?

Actually, she didn't know, and she didn't care. All she knew was that she didn't like the looks of what was going on with Adam. He was way too interested in those girls.

"Is that your girlfriend?" Miss Sweet asked Adam.

"No, just a friend," Adam said. "But would you please excuse me?"

"If you'll please come back," the redhead said in her sexiest voice.

"I will certainly try," Adam promised. "And

thank you both very much for the dance."

As he walked away, the redhead turned to Heather and said, "When was the last time you saw manners like that?"

"Yeah. It's like meeting a prince or something," Heather agreed.

Eve stood with her hands on her hips, waiting for her puppy to return to the table. As Adam made his way through the crowd, she glanced at Troy. "Go to the bathroom," she ordered him.

"Right here?" Troy asked.

Eve shot him a don't-get-smart-with-me look.

"Well, you're being so bossy, I wasn't sure!" Troy snapped. But he did as he was told, standing up to leave so that Eve could have Adam all to herself.

Adam smiled happily and took a seat at the table where Troy had been sitting.

Eve plopped down, too. Not smiling. Definitely not happy. More like grouchy and annoyed. In fact, more like furious. How come Adam was having so much fun—without her?

"You're not from Alaska," Eve said in an accusing voice. "Where'd you learn to dance like that? And there are no starving people, are there?"

Adam's face instantly took on a hurt expression. "Why are you suddenly so mad at me?" he asked.

"Don't change the subject!" Eve yelled.

"I've never lied to you," Adam said. "I've maybe let you believe things you wanted to believe, but I've never lied to you."

That couldn't be true, Eve thought. And even if it was, so what? Somehow, he was making her feel like a fool. Or at least she felt like she was missing something.

Something important.

"You think I'm some sort of sap?" she snapped.

"No. I admire you. I...I fell in love with you the first time I saw you," Adam said with such plain honesty that Eve's heart melted almost at once.

But she had one rule, one rule that had protected her her entire life. Never drop your guard. Never let anyone see a soft spot. Keep the walls up at all times.

So she wasn't going to fall for a line like that. No way.

Besides, it was obvious that he had been lying to her somehow. Pretending to be someone he wasn't.

How else could she explain the fact that he seemed...transformed? Suddenly he wasn't a nerd from the country anymore. Suddenly he spoke French and danced wonderfully and knew how to make beautiful women happy.

"I want you to stop lying to me!" Eve demanded. Ridiculously, her voice cracked. "I want to know exactly who you are and what you're really up to!"

"Then let me tell you the full truth about

myself," Adam said, his gaze drilled into hers. "It's incredible, but it's the truth."

"Okay, tell me," Eve said, nodding. She sat perfectly still and held her breath, waiting to hear Adam's whole story.

chapter ten

Adam took a deep breath.

Okay, he thought. I'll trust her and tell her everything. About the fallout shelter. About how my dad protected us from the atomic blast. And about not having ever been on the surface until a few days ago.

But just as he was trying to think of the best way to begin, a man ambled up to the table.

Adam recognized him. Cliff. The guy with the legs and body and hair that Eve liked. Her old boyfriend.

He was dressed all in black, Adam noticed. Slinky black pants, a black silk T-shirt, and a black alligator belt.

Bad timing, Adam thought. I wish he would just go away.

"Well, well, well," Cliff said in a mocking tone as he approached. "Don't we clean up nice?"

Adam stood up instantly. After all, that's what a gentleman did when another man approached the table, right?

Even if he *did* wish that Cliff would disappear.

Adam held out his hand to shake.

"Hello, Cliff, how are you this evening?" Adam asked.

Cliff barely returned the handshake. "Not bad," he said, quickly sitting down in Adam's chair. "But I *do* miss that green sport coat of yours," he added even more sarcastically.

"Excuse me, Cliff," Adam said, being polite but firm. "But that's my seat."

Cliff ignored the comment and turned his fake smile on Eve. "How about a drink at the bar?"

He's trying to get her back, Adam thought. He's here just to take her away from me.

Eve paused, glancing from Adam to Cliff for half a second. She seemed to be deciding something.

"Okay," Eve said, standing. Then she gave Adam a warning glance. "Don't do anything while I'm gone," she ordered him. "I'll be right back."

Cliff stood up too and shot a superior smile at Adam. Then he gestured to Adam's chair, now empty. "It's all yours," he said as he guided Eve away from the table toward the bar.

Adam sat down glumly and scowled. The evening wasn't working out the way he'd hoped. Not at all. He'd never planned to spend the whole evening wife-hunting *alone*. It just wasn't as much fun without Eve.

Nothing was as much fun without Eve.

And besides, he thought. What was she doing, going back to Cliff now, anyway? Hadn't she said that he was shallow? And that's why things never worked out?

And more important, didn't she want to hear what he was going to tell her? The truth about who he was and where he really came from?

Adam stared across the dance floor idly, until his gaze landed on a familiar face. Miss Sweet. She was sitting at a table on the far side of the room with Heather and some other guy—a handsome gentleman, Adam thought, who seemed more interested in Heather than anyone else.

I wish I'd gotten Miss Sweet's real name, Adam thought. It's silly to keep calling her Miss Sweet.

Miss Sweet smiled the minute she caught Adam's eye. Then she nudged Heather. Both women began smiling and waving coyly from across the room.

Adam let his gaze follow Miss Sweet's main features: her hair, her body, her legs.

Yes, he thought. They were nice features. But hair and bodies and legs didn't make up a whole person, did they?

All of a sudden, Adam stood up. He scanned the bar until he found Eve and Cliff. Then he headed straight toward them.

"So where is your new roommate, the model?" Eve was asking Cliff.

"You know, I don't know," Cliff was saying. "And looking at you, I don't care. It's been too long, Eve."

This was bad. Adam had to do something before things went too far between Cliff and Eve.

He strode up and planted himself beside Cliff. "Please excuse the interruption," he said. "But..."

"Oh, brother," Cliff muttered.

Adam looked past Cliff at Eve.

"Eve, I don't mean to be rude, and please excuse me, Cliff, but, Eve, isn't Cliff just a body with hair?"

"*What?*" Cliff shot Eve a furious glare.

"I'm sorry," Adam said, correcting himself. He had left something out. "And legs. Legs, body, and hair. Well, isn't he? And shallow as well?"

"*Shallow?*" Cliff repeated.

He sounded insulted, Adam thought. Totally insulted. But he was way too shallow to come across with anything more than raising his voice to convey anger and fury.

"Did you say *shallow*?" he repeated.

Eve stepped forward to try to keep things calm.

"Go home, Adam," she ordered him. "Just go back to your hotel."

"Yeah," Cliff chimed in, putting a firm hand on Adam's chest and shoving him. "Before I pound you."

"Cliff, I must warn you," Adam said firmly. "I know how to defend myself."

"Do you?"

Cliff pulled back his right fist and tried to throw a hard punch at Adam's face.

Adam's left arm came up quickly to block the punch. Just as his father had taught him.

In the shelter, Calvin had trained him thoroughly in boxing.

An instant later, Adam's right fist shot out with a quick jab to Cliff's mouth. The punch was strong enough, and fast enough, to snap Cliff's head back.

It wasn't a big punch, but it was very, very quick. Cliff clapped a hand to his jaw and glared at Adam. Adam kept his fists up.

Troy, Jason, and Jonathan watched from a few feet away, looking astonished.

Eve's face flushed. "Stop it, you two!" she yelled. She said it as if she expected to be obeyed.

"We shouldn't fight in here," Cliff muttered, rubbing his jaw.

Adam lowered his guard. "Yes, I agree."

After all, Adam thought, gentlemen don't fight in front of ladies. Right?

The minute Adam dropped his arms, Cliff swung at him again.

What a bad sport! Adam thought, shocked. He blocked the punch, then threw a quick left jab to Cliff's cheek, again snapping his head back.

Cliff staggered slightly, but he didn't fall. He looked stunned. And his face was already beginning to swell.

He pulled back one more time, ready to really let it fly at Adam this time. But before he could even release his punch, Adam popped him with a quick jab to the nose. Blood began to leak out of Cliff's left nostril.

"Ow! Man, oh, man! Don't break my nose!" Cliff reached up to his face and anxiously felt his nose.

Adam waited calmly. I'm happy to stop whenever you are, he thought. But he knew from experience that he shouldn't let his guard down too soon.

He wasn't going to be tricked. Not by someone like Cliff.

"Maybe we shouldn't fight at all," Cliff said sullenly. "It's pretty immature."

"It certainly is," Adam agreed like a gentleman. He lowered his guard again. "I agree with you completely."

"Eve?" Cliff said, his voice slightly shaky. "I'm leaving."

"I don't blame you!" She sounded furious.

Adam heard the anger in her voice. "Eve, I'm sorry." He turned to apologize.

Then, out of the corner of his eye, he saw Cliff coming after him one more time. Rearing back, trying to take another swing.

This is really too much! Adam thought angrily.

Spinning, he popped Cliff in the mouth. Cliff's lip split open. Blood now streamed from both of Cliff's nostrils, and from his mouth.

Cliff tried to cling to his last shred of dignity. "Well, good night, everyone," he said.

"I'm leaving, too," Eve said. She fixed Adam with an icy blue gaze for just a moment before turning away.

"But I..." Adam stammered.

This isn't what he wanted at all. This wasn't why he had come over to the bar.

He hadn't *meant* to start a fight. Or pound Cliff's face into hamburger. And he *definitely* had not meant to make Eve angry at him.

He was just doing what any man would do in the same situation. Defending his honor.

Eve turned back. "And tomorrow, maybe Troy will help you out with your life, or whatever it is you're doing. Because I *quit*!" she yelled.

Then she whirled around and marched out of

the club.

Adam felt his throat tighten up as he watched her walk away.

Then he heard Troy's voice behind him.

"If it makes you feel any better, she *always* quits. At everything," Troy said softly.

Adam nodded. He knew that already. He'd seen her quit in the baseball card shop, on his first day up above ground.

But it didn't help to know that about her. Not right now. Not when he really wanted her to come back.

It didn't help one bit.

chapter eleven

Eve sat in the living room of the house she shared with Troy. She had already changed into gray sweats and a T-shirt.

Now she was waiting.

Waiting for Troy to come home and give her the report.

When she finally heard his car in the driveway, she jumped up and rushed to the door.

She glanced at the clock. It was after midnight.

Man, she thought. She'd been pacing back and forth in the living room for two hours, wondering what happened after she left the club.

Wondering about Adam.

She flung the front door open before Troy

could even get his key in the lock.

"Did he go back to the hotel?" Eve demanded.

"Uh...he might have," Troy said, not exactly coming to the point. He dragged himself into the living room and tossed his keys down.

"What does that mean?" Eve asked. Grilling him.

"We did not leave together," Troy answered in a weary voice.

"Who did he leave with?" Her voice rose sharply.

"What's it to you?" Troy shot back. "I mean, seriously, you walked out on him."

"I've got a right to know," Eve snapped. "I set him up for this whole thing. He left with the dancers, didn't he?"

"Hey, you're the psychic. You tell me," Troy snapped.

"Those girls aren't right for him!" Eve cried.

"You can't run his *whole* life," Troy said, shrugging and kicking off his shoes. Then he headed down the hall, toward his bedroom.

No way, buddy, Eve thought. I'm not through with you!

"Where are you going?" she demanded.

"To bed."

"To bed?" She was outraged.

"Yeah. I'm not the one who's in love with the guy," Troy said.

"What? Now, hold on!" Eve protested, following Troy down the hall. "Wait just one minute!"

Troy didn't wait, though. He pushed into his bedroom and plopped down on the bed.

"In the first place," Eve argued, following him into his room, "I don't fall in love with weirdos I've only known for four days."

"Yes, you do," Troy said matter-of-factly.

"And I don't fall in love with grown men who collect baseball cards!" Eve screamed.

"No?"

"Or who lose it completely when they see the ocean! Or have perfect table manners!" she ranted on.

Troy sat and wrapped his arms around his knees. "You know, I asked him about that. And he said that good manners are a way we have of showing other people that we respect them. See, you'd eat like a slob if you were alone, but since another human being is present, you show that person respect by going to the *trouble* of having proper manners. I didn't know that. I thought it was a way of appearing superior."

Troy paused to let that sink in. Then he added, "Know what else he told me?"

Eve sat down on the end of his bed. "What?"

"He thinks that *I* am a gentleman and that *you* are a lady!"

Eve rolled her eyes. "Well, consider the

source," she said. "I don't even know what a lady is."

"Exactly!" Troy said, pointing a finger at her. "I thought a gentleman was somebody who owned horses. Turns out, the short and very simple definition of a gentleman or a lady is someone who always attempts to make the people around him or her feel as comfortable as possible. That's *it*. If you don't do that, nothing else matters. You're not a gentleman."

Eve sank down on Troy's bed. "Where did he get all that information?" she wondered aloud.

"From the oddest place," Troy answered. "His parents told him."

"So now I suppose he's trying to make those two dancers feel as comfortable as possible," she said wryly.

"He didn't leave with the dancers," Troy said carefully.

Whew! Eve thought. That's the best news I've had all night. She relaxed.

"Well...I admit it. I'm not sorry to hear that," she said.

Troy's face twisted slightly. As if he were breaking the punch line to her gently.

"He left with Sophie," he announced.

"*What?*" Eve jumped up off the bed. "Do not tell me that! Do not!"

"It's true," Troy said. "She swept him out the

door, whispering little French nothings into his ear."

"And you let him go?" Eve screamed.

What a traitor! she thought. How could her own roommate treat her so totally shabbily?

"You jerk!" she yelled at Troy.

"Me?" Troy sounded shocked that she could even dream of blaming him for this. "How, exactly, is this my fault?"

"How much do you think he knows about love? You don't have to be psychic to know the guy's never dated anyone before. He's ripe to get his heart broken. In fact, I'd be willing to bet he's never even been kissed!"

Troy's face flashed shock. Obviously, the idea had not even occurred to him.

"Yes! Believe me, I know!" Eve insisted. "I have this thing!"

"So what are you going to do?" Troy asked sarcastically. "Race over to Sophie's condo, kick in the door, and drag our boy home?"

"Yes! And you're going to come with me!" she yelled.

Troy shook his head. "No, I'm not!"

"Why not?"

"Because this is between you and Adam," he said. "And Sophie, of course."

Eve felt desperate. "Troy," she begged. "Please. Help me."

"Sorry," Troy said with a definite shake of his head.

"You creep!" Eve cried, spitting out the word. She slammed out of his room and grabbed her keys. She ran toward the front door.

She had to rescue innocent Adam from Sophie's clutches—before it was too late!

chapter twelve

Eve jammed her feet into shoes, and tore out the front door.

How could Troy be so irresponsible? she thought furiously.

Didn't he know that Adam was...special? That you couldn't just let him wander around on his own all night? Loose?

Of course, he wasn't wandering alone, Eve realized. That was the problem. He was with *her*.

Sophie.

Greedy, selfish Sophie.

He deserved someone better than that. Someone who could take care of him, Eve thought as she ran to her car.

Her hands shook as she fumbled with her car keys, trying to jam them into the lock.

"Come on! Come on!" she mumbled.

Finally she got the car door open. She jumped inside, kicking a few pieces of fast-food garbage aside, and stuck the key in the ignition.

"Hi!" a voice at the passenger-side window said.

Adam!

The sound of his voice, out of the blue like that, startled Eve so much that she screamed. All the bottled-up emotions of the past few hours came blasting out of her in one gigantic shriek of shock and surprise.

She flung open the driver-side door and tried to leap out of the car. But her nerves were totally jangled by then. And there was too much trash on the car floor.

She tripped and went sprawling on the cement, falling on her hands and knees. She let out another scream of pain.

Three or four dogs began barking from different parts of the neighborhood.

"Eve!" Adam cried, racing around the car to help her.

Adam! she wanted to cry. Where have you been? Why are you running around L.A. with a woman who couldn't care less about you? Don't you see you'll just get hurt?

But she was so wired, so emotionally wrung out, she couldn't say it that way. She couldn't turn her emotions off. All her frustration flooded out at him.

"*Scare me, why don't you*! You stupid idiot!" she screamed.

"I'm really sorry!" Adam said helplessly.

"What are you doing here, anyway?" she cried. "You're supposed to be over on San Vicente Boulevard, getting your heart broken by that man-eater Sophie!"

"I know...and I'm very sorry," Adam said. He really did sound truly and utterly apologetic.

"Well, you *should* be!" Eve yelled. Just to be yelling. "Thanks to you, my heart is in my neck!"

"What?" Adam looked blank.

Eve wasn't going to explain it. "Good night!" she announced, marching back toward her house with a limp.

Adam followed her, trying to make things better.

"Eve, if you'll let me, I can—"

"Look!" she snapped. "I'm limping! How attractive is that? What if this is for life?"

"I know first aid!" Adam declared as they entered the house.

"Well," Eve said, shooting him a sideways glance, "you'd *better*!"

Eve finally managed to calm herself down. Only after that was she able to sit down on the couch, *stay* down, and let Adam take care of her.

He fetched some alcohol from the medicine cabinet in the bathroom. Then he knelt beside her in the living room and began swabbing at the scrape on her knee.

When she fell, her sweatpants had torn clear through. But the hole wasn't very big. He was having a hard time getting enough alcohol on the wound through the small opening.

"Wait a minute," Eve said. She reached down, grabbed the torn piece of fabric, and gave it a good rip to expose more of her leg. "There."

"Thanks," Adam said, smiling up at her.

Their eyes locked for a second, and Eve almost softened enough to smile back.

Look at him, she thought. He's so tender. So concerned. I could just die.

If I did that sort of thing.

Adam held the back of her calf in one hand and swabbed at the scrape with the other.

It stung a little. Involuntarily, Eve flinched.

"Steady. Steady," Adam encouraged her. "It's going to be all right in no time."

He might just be the sweetest guy I've ever met, Eve thought, watching the top of his head.

He leaned in close and blew on the wound to make the antiseptic dry more quickly.

Eve shivered, feeling his hand on her leg, his breath on her knee, his lips so close to her skin....

"I went to Sophie's and she was very hospitable," Adam told her, glancing up.

"Hospitable? Is *that* what you call it?" Eve cracked. She gave a harsh laugh.

Adam didn't seem to notice her sarcasm. "But it just wasn't where I wanted to be. So I left as politely as I could and found a taxi," he went on. "I asked the driver to drop me here instead of at the hotel. There's a song Perry Como sings called 'On the Street Where You Live.' You know it?"

"Sort of," Eve said. She was getting a funny feeling in her stomach.

"Sing it to me," she commanded softly.

Adam cleared his throat and began to half-sing, half-talk the lyrics. "'All at once am I/ Several stories high/ Knowing I'm/ On the street/ Where you live.' It's about a young man who is overjoyed just to be standing in front of this young woman's house," he explained in a near whisper.

Wow, Eve thought, staring into his eyes.

Just...wow.

Suddenly she was dying to kiss him. To feel his lips pressed against hers.

Reaching down, she gently took hold of Adam's collar and drew him up to her.

He kissed her tenderly. A long, warm, loving kiss that was both the gentlest and the sexiest thing she'd ever experienced.

Finally it was over.

Eve sat still for a moment, catching her breath. Then she looked at him questioningly.

"Adam...dumb question," she began, "but—humor me. Have you ever kissed anyone before?"

"No."

"But...how is that possible?" she asked, sitting up straighter.

This was the question she *really* wanted answered.

How could he possibly *be* the way he was?

Adam perched beside her on the sofa. "I've been wanting to do this all night," he said. "To tell you the truth."

Okay, Eve thought. Here we go.

Adam took a deep breath. "See, in 1962, when the bomb was dropped on Los Angeles, my parents were in our fallout shelter," he began. "That's where I was born. We only survived because it was a huge shelter as fallout shelters go. My father worked on it, secretly, for years. When he had to, he used contractors, but always from out of state and always for just a portion of the job. He told them it was a secret government experiment done through CalTech. My dad's not a liar, but he felt in this case he had no choice. Of course it had to be a secret, because we had just enough supplies to last three people thirty-five years. That's also why I have no brothers or sisters. The air vent was the really tricky part," he added earnestly, "but Dad was able to cut into a flood control sewer—so it all worked out."

Oh, no, Eve thought. It was just what she'd been afraid of. Deep in her heart.

He's crazy.

He's totally and completely schizoid. Crazy.

Bottom line...nuts.

Her heart sank. She felt like bursting into tears, for the first time in about twenty years.

What was she doing? Sitting there, falling in love with a guy who...who thought he'd spent his whole life in a bomb shelter?

Nope. She wasn't going to do this. Not Eve. She wasn't going to get sucked in like this.

She steeled herself, then put a calm hand on Adam's shoulder.

"Adam?"

"Yes, Eve?"

"I want you to go back to the hotel now," she said softly. Not an order this time. A request. "I'll call you a cab."

"Of course," Adam said, standing. "I shouldn't be over here at this hour. Will you forgive me?"

"Of course." Eve led him to the door. "And I'll see you in the morning. In the lobby at the hotel." She opened the front door before asking, "Do you mind waiting outside for the taxi?"

"Not at all," Adam replied, always the gentleman. "And Eve, thank you for tonight...and for the kiss. My first."

"My pleasure," she said, biting her lip.

"It was at least as good as the sky," Adam reported.

"*Really*. Okay," Eve said, trying to stay calm.

"And I think better than the ocean," Adam went on. When he caught the stunned expression on her face, he added, "I'm serious!"

"Neat," Eve said, closing the door quickly. "Good night."

"Good night," Adam called from outside.

Eve locked the door. She was trying hard not to cry.

Suddenly, she felt incredibly sad. Sadder than she'd ever felt in her life.

As if she'd just lost—forever—the most important person she'd ever known.

Even if he was still only on the other side of the door.

chapter thirteen

"Why couldn't she come? Explain it to me again, please, Troy," Adam asked.

Adam glanced over at Troy, who was sitting beside him in the rented refrigerated truck. He was waiting to hear a reasonable explanation for why only Troy, and not Eve, had shown up in the lobby of the hotel that morning.

"Her knee," Troy said. "It's still bothering her. From the fall last night."

"Oh." Adam nodded. "I thought you said she had something important to do for a friend."

"Well, that, too." Troy said.

"Has she seen a doctor?" Adam asked, worrying about her knee.

"Yes, actually, she has," Troy said.

But Adam noticed a strange note creeping into his voice.

Troy's hiding something, he thought. *Or not exactly telling me the truth.*

But Adam couldn't figure out why.

Maybe it was Eve's knee. Maybe she was more hurt than Troy wanted to admit.

Or maybe it was something else.

Adam wanted to ask for more details. But the traffic on the boulevard was heavy—and he was new to driving. He shoved the gearshift lever into third, and tried to let out the clutch. The truck lurched forward, almost rear-ending another car.

"Man, Adam!" Troy shouted, gripping the passenger-side armrest. "Take it easy!"

Adam immediately steered the truck to the side of the road and turned off the engine. "Wait a minute!" he shouted.

"Whoops," Troy said quickly. "Sorry. I know— I'm not supposed to shout. I'm so sorry."

"No." Adam shook his head. That wasn't it. "There's a malt shop back there!" he said. "I'll be right back!"

Finally! Adam thought. The landmark he'd been looking for.

If it was the right one, then he wouldn't be lost anymore. He'd be able to gather up all the supplies he'd been buying for his parents and take them to the fallout shelter.

Adam leaped out of the car and hurried back down the block, his face glowing in anticipation.

He read the sign over the door: MOM'S MALT SHOP.

Yes! That was the place!

"I'm not lost anymore!" Adam cried. He felt almost light-headed with relief.

He tried the front door of the malt shop. It opened. He peered inside.

The man who had built a shrine near the bomb shelter's elevator was still there. Praying.

Okay, Adam thought, closing the door again. This is the right place. I know where I am now.

With a smile on his face, he hurried back to the refrigerator truck.

"Okay, Troy!" Adam said, hopping up behind the wheel again. "Let's get those all-beef frozen patties now!"

Troy sort of cleared his throat.

"How about we check with Eve first?" Troy suggested.

"You bet!" Adam agreed, beaming.

Why not? he thought. He was happy to go along with any plan that involved being with Eve.

It took almost an hour to reach Eve's house from the malt shop. By the time they pulled up out front, there were two other cars parked at the curb.

I wonder if she has visitors, Adam thought, glancing at the cars. If she does, I'll have to wait to tell her about the malt shop.

And to ask her to come meet my mom and dad.

Because that's what he wanted—more than anything else. To introduce her to his parents.

"Mom and Dad," he would say. "I want you to meet Eve Cosovak."

And then they would understand the rest—without being told. That she was the most wonderful woman in the world. That he was hoping to spend more time with her. That he hadn't given up yet on the idea of getting her to fall in love with him.

What a day! Adam thought as he parked the refrigerator truck in the driveway. Everything was falling into place at last.

He'd finally found his way back home. And last night, he'd finally told Eve the truth. About his life underground.

Now, maybe, she'd understand the reason he was...different.

He bounded up the front walk and into Eve's house, bursting with happiness.

For some reason, Troy followed slowly behind.

Eve was standing in the living room, almost as if she had been waiting for Adam to arrive.

"Hi, Eve!" he greeted her.

Then he noticed that she wasn't alone. She *did*

have visitors. A kind-looking woman in a red suit stood next to Eve, smiling.

"Hi, Adam," Eve said. "This is, uh..."

"I'm Dr. Adele Aron," the woman said, introducing herself.

"How do you do?" Adam said, shooting Eve a questioning glance.

What was going on? he wondered. Did the visitors have something to do with him?

"I'm with the Family Services Department," the woman explained. "Eve tells me you've been living in a bomb shelter all your life."

Oh, no, Adam thought. It *did* have something to do with him.

Eve had told other people about him.

"It's a fallout shelter," Adam corrected the woman. "Actually, my mother told me not to mention that to anyone until I could...well..."

Trust them, Adam thought. But it was too late now for that.

"Adam," the woman said, "I'd like to introduce you to two of my associates—Mr. Brown and Mr. Shaw."

Two very large men in polo shirts and khakis stepped out of Eve's kitchen—where they seemed to have been hiding. They looked sort of like bodyguards.

Or the kind of men who hauled people off to the loony bin, Adam thought.

His heart began to race. How come Eve had told so many strangers about the fallout shelter? And why had those men been hiding in the kitchen? And why was Troy slinking over to the corner with a horrible guilty expression on his face? Like he'd led Adam into a trap?

"We want you to come with us," Adele Aron said. "So we can talk about your experiences."

"Come where?" Adam asked.

"My office," Dr. Aron answered.

"For how long?" Adam asked.

Maybe he hadn't been on the surface very long, he thought. But he wasn't a complete idiot. He'd read books...about people being locked up....

"Well," Dr. Aron answered, "that depends."

No, Adam thought. I can't let this happen.

"I thank you very much for the invitation, but I'm quite busy today. Perhaps I could see you tomorrow," he said.

Eve stepped forward and put a hand on his arm.

"Adam...you should go with these people," she said. "It's the best thing. The best thing for *you*. I promise."

Adam looked at the worried but loving expression on Eve's face.

She didn't understand. About the shelter. About his life. She didn't realize that everything he'd told her was true.

And now, because she cared about him, she was

trying to have him locked up.

He felt defeated.

"All right, Eve," he said. "If you say so."

"I do," Eve said firmly.

Adam turned to Adele Aron, who he guessed was actually a psychiatrist, although she hadn't specifically said so.

"Could I please just go home?" he asked her. "I know where home is now, and I promise not to bother any of you ever again."

"Let's talk first, Adam," Dr. Aron replied.

"Yes, ma'am," Adam said with a small sigh.

The two burly men stepped forward, as if they were there to make sure Adam didn't give anyone any trouble. One of them opened the front door and motioned for Adam to step out.

"Good-bye, Adam," Troy said softly from his corner.

"Good-bye."

Adam glanced at Eve, waiting. Waiting for her to say something. Anything.

At least good-bye.

She just turned away, not meeting his eyes.

"You'll be hearing from me," Dr. Aron told Eve. Then she followed Adam out the front door, pulling it closed behind her.

As soon as they were out the door, Eve rushed to the window to watch them leave.

She saw Adam take a few slow steps along the front walk with the two men flanking him, and Dr. Aron behind.

Then, all at once, at just the right moment to catch them off guard, she saw him bolt.

Breaking away. Running.

Eve gasped.

"Oh, no!" she cried, racing out the front door. Troy was right behind her.

To her surprise, Adam was a pretty good sprinter. And he was certainly in much better shape than the two oversized lugs who had come along as muscle power.

He leaped over some bushes and dashed down a driveway between two houses. He was giving the big guys a serious workout.

Dr. Aron was already dialing her cell phone.

"They'll catch him," she told Eve calmly. "Don't worry." Then, into the phone, she said, "This is Dr. Aron. I've got a 720 in Santa Monica and I'm going to need a squad car."

"No!" Eve cried. "Not the police! Don't call them!"

"I have to," Dr. Aron insisted. "What's the address here?"

No way. Eve wasn't going to help this woman put Adam in jail!

She quickly stepped sideways, covering up the house number on the wall by the front door. At the same time, Troy tried to grab Dr. Aron's cell phone away.

"What are you doing?" Dr. Aron shouted. "Stop that! Stop it!"

Troy struggled with the woman. Dr. Aron pulled a hunk of his hair. Hard. Troy clawed back at her, almost knocking off her glasses.

The fight was about to turn ugly, when suddenly Adam appeared from around the side of the house. Still running.

The sight of him startled everyone.

"Here!" he called to Eve, tossing her something as he jogged toward the truck. "The key to my hotel room! I want you to have my baseball cards! And be sure to pay my bill!"

Then he jumped behind the wheel of the refrigerator truck.

"Adam, you really shouldn't try to drive that truck!" Troy called.

"Bye, Troy!" Adam replied as he started the engine.

"Bye!" Troy called back.

Adam put the truck in reverse and began to back down the driveway. But in his hurry he smacked into one of the cars parked near the curb.

Adam pulled forward, then back, doing more damage in the process. He even drove the truck down the sidewalk a short way, clipping two more parked cars as he struggled to steer the truck.

Finally, he zoomed out onto the street and roared off.

Eve stood on the lawn, staring after him. He was free!

But what about me? Eve wondered. I'm never going to see him again.

He's crazy, she reminded herself. I don't need him in my life.

So then why do I feel so totally sad?

chapter fourteen

"**M**om? Dad? I'm home!" Adam called, racing into the bomb shelter an hour later.

Adam's parents were in the breakfast room, drinking tea and reading books. The minute they heard Adam's voice, they jumped up and ran to greet their son.

Helen threw her arms around him, hugging and kissing him as if he'd been gone for years. As if he were returning from a war— and she hadn't been sure he'd come back alive.

Yes, Adam thought. It is sort of like I've been fighting a battle of some kind.

He let them hug him as long as they wanted.

When his mother finally let go, he turned back

toward the exit hatchway. He motioned for the man from the malt shop to step forward.

"I've gotten all the supplies," Adam explained to his parents. "Almost everything we need. And this nice man..."

Adam wasn't sure of the man's name. But the guy had been so pleasant every time Adam passed through the malt shop. He kept treating Adam as if he were a savior of some kind.

"This nice man..." Adam repeated.

"Archbishop Melker," the guy filled in his name.

"...and his church group have volunteered to help us bring the supplies down. But we've got to hurry."

Helen frowned, hearing the note of urgency in Adam's voice.

"Are you in trouble, son?" she asked.

"I think I'm being chased by a psychiatrist," Adam explained.

"A psychiatrist!" His mother was aghast.

"It happens," the guy from the malt shop said matter-of-factly.

"My goodness! How bad is it up there?" Helen asked.

"Horrible," the guy replied. "Just horrible."

Eve carefully put the room key in the lock at the Hollywood Holiday Inn. She stepped quietly into Adam's room.

"He's not here," she announced to Troy, who had followed her inside. "I knew he wouldn't be here."

"Yeah, but maybe we can find something. A clue about where he's gone," Troy said.

"Exactly," Eve said. She marched over to his dresser and opened one of the drawers.

Wow, she thought, eyeing his neatly folded shirts, socks, and underwear. It reminded her of her mother's dresser—when Eve was a kid. The way everything was so carefully put away.

She opened all four drawers, searching for the cigar box with the baseball cards.

It wasn't there.

She glanced at Troy, who was standing beside a night table. Idly, he opened the drawer on the nightstand.

"What about this?" he asked, pulling out a coated cardboard box.

"That's it!" Eve cried, dashing over.

"What do you want to do with it?" Troy asked.

"Give it back to him."

What else was there to do? Eve thought. The box and the cards belonged to Adam. She didn't want his money. She just wanted him to be okay.

"And if we can't find him?" Troy asked.

Not find him?

Eve felt her brow knit with tension at the very

thought of that idea.

"We'll find him," she said firmly, beginning to search the room again. "We *have* to find him."

She zoomed into the bathroom, then stopped short.

Wow—again. His comb, brush, and toothpaste were precisely lined up on the vanity. His socks had clearly been washed in the sink and were neatly hung up to dry.

Eve picked up the toothpaste and stared at it lovingly. Adam had very carefully squeezed the paste from the bottom, just the way her mother always *wanted* Eve to.

It was strange—an odd brand of toothpaste. Something called Ipana, in a yellow tube.

Eve's eyes began to fill with tears.

"Hey, Eve?" Troy said, coming into the bathroom. Then he noticed that her eyes were wet and her lip was trembling. "What's wrong?"

"I don't know," she moaned, trying not to cry. "Everything's so...so neat. It's all just so...so unbelievably *dear*." Tears began to trickle down her cheeks.

"Listen," Troy said, "I found something."

She looked up questioningly.

"See these?" he went on. "I found them in the box with the baseball cards. They're stock certificates, Eve. IBM. AT&T. Polaroid."

Eve glanced at Troy, then back at the stock certificates. Then back at Troy again.

She caught the this-is-important look on his face.

"Check this out," she said, handing him the tube of toothpaste and trading him for the stock certificates.

Troy stared at the tube of Ipana, his eyes growing wide.

"Eve?" he said. "This toothpaste...it's...it's old. It's from 1961!"

Eve glanced up. Frozen. Her heart was pounding too hard to say anything for an instant.

She nodded, then handed the stock certificates back to Troy. "These are even older," she said softly, trying not to totally freak out.

But she couldn't ignore the facts. The facts that seemed to be hitting her square in the face.

Maybe Adam had been telling her the truth. About the bomb shelter. About living underground his whole life.

Troy rushed back into the bedroom and began dialing the phone. In two minutes, he had his friend Jason on the line. Jason was a stockbroker.

Quickly Troy described the stock certificates and asked him what they were worth.

"They were purchased in 1958 and '59," Troy explained. "Ten thousand shares of each."

Troy listened a moment. "Okay, thanks," he said, hanging up.

Eve took one look at Troy's face and knew what he was going to say.

He was going to tell her that they'd made a horrible mistake.

That they should have believed Adam.

"He's worth millions, Eve," Troy announced. "Millions upon millions upon millions! The cards. The stocks. The clothes. The toothpaste! The guy was on the level, Eve—and you blew it! A man walks into your life who is the kindest, most polite, honest, trustworthy, incredibly rich guy you have ever met in your life! And what do you do?"

"Have him committed," Eve said with a groan.

"Is this the ultimate Eve Cosovak mistake? Or can we take it to another level?" Troy ranted on. "Let's think! There must be a way to make this even *more* terrible!"

Eve cringed. Yeah, okay. Troy was right.

She ruined everything good that ever happened to her. Quit every job. Dumped every guy. Infuriated almost every friend.

But this...this was not my fault, she thought. How was I supposed to know that Adam's wacko story was true?

Suddenly her eyes lit up.

Maybe...just maybe...it wasn't too late.

Maybe she could still find him.

"Wait a minute. He said today that he knew

where home was," Eve announced.

"So?" Troy didn't get the point.

"So he never said that before," Eve explained. "When did he find out? Where did you go this morning? Did anything excite him? Did he see or recognize anything unusual?"

Troy thought for a second. Then he snapped his fingers. "I know where it was!" he exclaimed. He grabbed the stock certificates and the cigar box and headed for the door.

"Where?" Eve called.

"You drive, I'll give directions" was all Troy would say.

By the time they reached the San Fernando Valley, it was nightfall. A huge silvery moon hung in the sky, the only purely beautiful object in sight on the run-down, seedy street.

"You've got to be kidding," Eve muttered when she saw the malt shop. "Here?"

"This is it," Troy announced, shaking his head. "This is where he jumped out of the truck like a maniac."

Okay, Eve thought. Whatever it took to find Adam, that's what she was willing to do.

She pulled on the door, but it was locked. Locked up tight.

"Anyone in there?" she yelled. She pounded her fist on the glass.

No answer. Nothing.

She tried to peer in the windows, but they were painted black. She couldn't see a thing inside.

And there wasn't a soul in sight.

"It can't be here," Eve muttered. "Why would you put a bomb shelter under a malt shop?"

Troy shrugged.

"None of this stuff was here in 1962," he said. "The Valley was mostly small homes and fruit orchards then. Who knows what was here when the bomb shelter was first built. You know?"

Eve yanked on the door again. Hoping. Maybe it would open this time.

But it didn't.

"I want to go home." Eve sighed.

"Yeah," Troy agreed half heartedly. He slung an arm around Eve's shoulders. "Let's go home and wait. That's all we can do. Wait—and hope. Maybe he'll call."

chapter fifteen

Adam stood on the street corner, fishing small coins out of his pocket and plopping them into the pay phone. Then he punched in the number that he'd written down on his palm.

Eve's number.

The phone in Troy and Eve's house rang four times before the machine picked up.

"Hi," Troy's voice said on the outgoing message. "Troy and Eve are out, so leave a message. And if you want to leave a number, don't say it fast! I hate that! Say it slow. Thank you."

BEEP.

Adam stood there silently, not knowing what to do next.

He'd never talked to an answering machine before. He never even knew that they existed until a day ago.

But he really, desperately, didn't want to go back to living in the bomb shelter without at least saying good-bye.

"Uh, Eve...this is Adam," he said finally. "Look, I just wanted to thank you for everything you did for me. And I wanted to tell you that I...uh...that I wish so many good things for you. I wish so hard that all of your dreams come true." He paused. "Bye," he said after a long while.

Then he hung up.

Now what? Adam wondered. Back to the fallout shelter?

For how long this time?

His father was determined to lock the doors again, for their own protection. And he was talking about setting the timers for ten years.

Even though the radiation was gone, Calvin wanted to make sure that nothing horrible from the surface—no mutants, no diseases—could contaminate them underground.

Adam stood by the phone booth. Ten years seemed like a very long time.

A tired, lonely feeling crept over him. He just didn't seem to care what happened next. Didn't care whether he saw the sky, or the ocean, or petted a dog, or learned to drive a car....

Or anything.

Without a wife—no, without *Eve*—life seemed, well, meaningless.

He took a deep breath and turned back toward the malt shop.

All of a sudden, a small, dirty Ford Geo cruised past him on the street.

And then, to his amazement, Adam heard his name being called. Called by the woman he loved with all his heart and soul.

He whirled around. Eve!

She was jumping out of her car, running toward him. She had been clutching his cigar box full of baseball cards and stock certificates, but it flew out of her hands as she leaped from the passenger seat.

Adam saw it fall. And all the baseball cards scatter. But he didn't care.

All he wanted was to be in her arms, holding her, kissing her….

He raced toward her, pulling her close to him. Her lips felt so soft….

He couldn't believe he was letting himself go this way. Kissing a young lady so…so aggressively, and in public.

But he couldn't stop himself. He didn't *want* to stop himself. He loved her so much, he just lost control.

Eve seemed to love him pretty much, too, because she wrapped her foot around his leg.

"Hello!" Troy commented, jumping out of the car. "I'm not sure this is allowed in the Valley!"

Then he raced around on the sidewalk and street, picking up the precious baseball cards and stock certificates before they blew away.

"Mom? Dad?" Adam called to his parents. He didn't want them to be startled when he walked in with a new friend.

Helen and Calvin were at the breakfast table again, waiting for Adam to return.

Calvin held the timing device in his hands. He was tinkering with it. Trying to set it for ten years.

"I'd like you to meet Miss Eve Cosovak," Adam said proudly. He led Eve forward.

Helen and Calvin both stared with their mouths open.

This is just what I've been hoping for, Adam realized. This moment. When I could bring the woman I love to meet my parents.

Eve stepped forward and offered her hand.

"How do you do, Mrs. Webber?" she said. "Mr. Webber?"

Helen and Calvin sputtered and stammered in their surprise.

Adam smiled. He could read his mother's face perfectly well. She was thinking: A woman? Has my son already met a young woman?

"Hello," Helen finally managed to say. Then

she snapped into her usual good-manners mode. "Please excuse us! We...we haven't entertained a guest in...um..."

"Some time," Calvin finished her sentence. He coughed and cleared his throat.

"What can I offer you, Eve?" Helen asked, trying to be a good hostess.

But Adam held up his hand. "Mom—Eve and I have to go," he said.

"What? Go where? You just got here, Adam."

"I can't explain it now," Adam said. "I just came to introduce Eve to you. And now I want you to set the locks for two months. You have more than enough of everything. Then we'll be back to get you."

"But—but I don't understand," Calvin said. His voice was bewildered.

"Dad, I'm asking you to trust me without understanding why," Adam replied gently but firmly.

Calvin blinked. "Of course, son," he said after a moment.

"Of course," Helen echoed.

Eve stared in astonishment.

"They *are* wonderful parents!" she exclaimed, gazing at Adam with even more adoration.

"Eve, I hope I'm not being nosy," Helen said gently, "but are you Adam's friend? Or his beau?"

Adam felt his face flush—with pride.

"I'm his beau," Eve said with a soft smile.

Helen's eyes filled with tears as she reached out to give Eve a warm hug.

They were tears of happiness, Adam decided, seeing the smile on his mother's face.

"I'm also from Pasadena," Eve added. It wasn't strictly true. But Adam had told her it would make them even happier.

And of course it worked. Helen began to sob with joy.

Adam felt his own throat begin to choke up. He was so happy, he thought he'd burst.

I know how you feel, Mom, he thought, gazing at Eve. Everything I've ever wanted has come true.

He reached out and took Eve's hand. It made him shiver just to look at her—the woman he loved more than anyone in the world.

There was just one thing left to do. One thing that would make everything complete…

chapter sixteen

That night was a turning point in Adam's life.
Eve knew it.

That night, Adam could have chosen between
her and his parents.

But he refused to do it.

Eve admired the fact that he couldn't turn away
from his mother and father, who had taught him
everything he knew. Given him everything. And
most of all, sacrificed thirty-five years of their lives
to keep him safe from an atomic bomb. Even if
that bomb had never been dropped.

But he couldn't give her up, either!

He made that totally clear.

So together, the two of them came up with a

plan. A plan to bring his parents to the surface.

"First," Adam said, "we have to create a world that they can be comfortable in."

"Good idea," Eve agreed. "But how?"

"We'll have their house rebuilt for them—exactly the way it used to be," Adam said. "But somewhere nicer. Somewhere that's still as beautiful as the Valley used to be."

"All it takes is money," Eve said, smiling at him. "In fact, it's truly amazing what you can get done when you have unlimited funds. All you have to say is 'I don't care what it costs.' And then, of course, you've got to mean it. Which no one ever does."

Luckily, Eve knew that Adam truly *didn't* care what it cost. Why should he? His stock certificates were worth enough money to make a lot of miracles happen. So he was able to get his parents' new house built in two months.

And he was considerate and loving enough, when it came to his parents, to think of everything. He had the house situated on a private road with a gate, so that nothing too outrageous—nothing from the 1990s—could make its way inside.

"Okay, Mom. Dad. Time to go home," Adam said, when the house was ready and the time locks had opened again.

Then he and Eve drove the Webbers to their

new home in a beautifully restored 1962 car, with darkened windows. That way, Helen and Calvin wouldn't see anything shocking or disturbing along the way.

When Helen Webber finally stepped outside and saw the sky again for the first time in thirty-five years, she gasped.

But that was nothing. Not compared to her reaction—and Calvin's—when Adam showed them all the modern conveniences in their new house.

Eve giggled privately, watching them race through the house, taking it all in.

A microwave. A VCR. A large-screen TV. And most amazing of all, a home computer.

"This is great, Adam!" Helen exclaimed after taking the tour of the whole house. "But where is *your* bedroom?"

Eve glanced at Adam and smiled.

"I won't be living here," Adam told his mother gently. "Eve and I eloped. We're married."

It didn't take more than a millisecond for a huge smile to spread across Helen's face.

"That's wonderful!" she cried, hugging her new daughter-in-law. "Calvin—they're married!" she called to her husband out on the new patio.

"That's wonderful!" Calvin said. He shook Adam's hand heartily, beaming.

There was only one thing that concerned Eve.

Adam's father was *still* worried about the Russians. He still thought the Russians had dropped the bomb, and that the Cold War was still going on.

And he seemed to wince every time Adam mentioned Eve's last name. Cosovak.

"It's not a Russian name, is it?" Calvin asked as they stood on the back patio.

"No. It's Ukrainian," Adam explained. He cleared his throat and took Calvin by the arm. Eve stood aside and listened.

"Dad, I want you to sit down," Adam began.

When Calvin was seated in a lawn chair, Adam went on. "I don't know how to tell you this, Dad. There was no bomb. A plane crashed into our backyard. I looked it up in old newspapers."

Calvin stared at his son. "You're...you're sure?" he asked.

"Positive," Adam said. "And there's more, Dad. The Soviet Union collapsed. The Cold War is over."

Calvin narrowed his eyes. "That's what everybody believes?"

"Yes. It's true."

"My gosh, those commies are brilliant!" Calvin said, jumping up. "You've got to hand it to 'em! 'No, we didn't drop any bombs! Oh, yes, our evil empire has collapsed!' Give me a break!"

Eve and Adam exchanged glances.

She saw Adam shake his head, and knew exactly what he was thinking.

If Calvin wanted to go on believing that the Russians were fooling everyone, why not let him? It probably wouldn't hurt anything.

Adam took Eve's hand and led her back through the house. Then the two of them stood on the front steps, gazing at the sunset over the crest of a hill lined with trees. The smell of orange blossoms drifted toward them from a nearby grove.

"I've never seen a son who did more for his parents in my life," Eve said, putting her arm lovingly around Adam's waist.

Adam shrugged. "This is simply how things work," he replied. "First the parents take care of the children—and then the children take care of the parents. Historically, that's how it's always worked. And it always will be that way."

Always will be that way? I sure hope so, Eve thought.

But before she could say anything, Adam bent down and kissed her with such tenderness that her heart melted again. And again. And again.

You're so sweet, Eve thought. The sweetest man alive.

And from then on, whenever Adam talked about the past as if things were still the way they used to be, Eve just smiled.

You can't really re-create the past, she thought.

But you can try to make the future a little better. That was Adam's dream.

And why spoil it? It was such a wonderful dream.

In fact, it was starting to be Eve's dream too!